The Voyage Of

The

Amelia Mary

By Lord R.e. Taylor

©2024 Shadowlight Publishing

Ipswich, Queensland

ISBN 978-1-7636761-9-0

There are mysteries that people, since the beginning of humankind, have been trying to figure out. The one that lingers the most, especially in the 22nd Century is that there may be another Earth on the opposite side of the Sun. The story is that Earth is a twin planet and that the other Earth is in the same orbit and is traveling at the same speed as Earth, so it would be impossible for observatories on our planet ever to see… or know conclusively if that planet exists. That is why, in 2075, the World Space Agency decided to send a ship to find out one way or the other.

Captains Samantha Young and Urula Mombassa were chosen to command the flight. Dr. Henry Louis-Hart was the science officer, medical officer Doctor Janet Giovanni, the linguistics officer, Lieutenant Asianne and Lieutenant Kevin Kiselow was chosen as the chief engineer. Although Kiselow was the youngest in the crew, in his short life he had more space experience than most men would at three times his age. There was also a crew of forty enlisted men and women who would perform the actual work aboard the ship.

On December 31, 2174, the W.S.S. Amelia Mary was prepped at a base in Western Siberia. The ship was named after Amelia Earhart, a female aviator from the 1900s who had the nerve to try what no one else could and she died in the process.

At 7:00 P.M. all the crew were taken to the ship and strapped in. It was going to be a long trip… exactly one year, and training and preparation for the mission had been going on for the last two years, so waiting a few hours to launch wasn't too much to ask.

They did their system checks, and everything was okay, but other than that they just waited. Finally, the last mandatory wait was over, and they were told that the launch would be in two minutes. For the crew, those last two minutes before takeoff seemed to stretch on forever.

Finally, a voice came over the radio. It was counting down for the last seconds and it wished them all a happy new year, as the audio finished, the engines kicked in, the ship started vibrating and the sound of a thousand thunderstorms filled the cabin. Then, slowly, the Amelia Mary lifted from the ground, faster and faster until the sound barrier was far behind them, as were the entire crew's thoughts and fears of traveling into space.

In less than 10 minutes, the Amelia Mary was in an orbit 350 miles above the

Earth. The plan was for the ship and crew to orbit the planet a few times... three to be exact—and then break orbit and head into space. The difference was that this time, the ship was not going to travel too far from Earth, as the entire Mission was to investigate if there was a twin Earth in the same orbit as ours.

It was scheduled for a one-hour burn of its engines and then to stop dead in the place where the planet had been predetermined by a revolutionary, Noble Prize-winning, scientist several years ago. Supposedly, the ship would stop at a distance of 750,000 miles from Earth and it performed exactly as it should.

The crew watched the Earth travel away from them at 67,000 miles an hour. It hit them all at the same time that their homes were fading away into the blackness of space. Some of them cheered and others just stared in wonder without saying a word. For all of them, it was a moment of elation yet also an uneasy anticipation and an understandable fear of the unknown, as they were all on a voyage that no one had ever taken before to find something that no one had ever seen.

It wasn't too long before Captain Samantha Young looked out of the window and looked back at Earth, and it was no more than a blue disk no bigger than the size of a ten-cent piece. "Look," she said. "The Earth suddenly looks so insignificant and so small. Yet it provides us with so much, how stupid we are destroying our beautiful planet and instead of love and compassion for each other we are so filled with envy and hate."

Captain Mombassa. She had been involved in several local wars while living in Africa. "I have witnessed humans doing the most unspeakable things to each other," he said. "Watching innocent people killed for no reason… that is something the leaders of all governments should have to do… watch their people die."

Everyone agreed and as they watched the world, they knew it had become that small ten cent disk, they all agreed that on the Amelia Mary that all would be harmony, and there would be no confrontations of any kind on the ship.

Since there were all mainly differing nationalities and races on board, that was a step that had to be taken, and it had to be unanimous, and it was. The Amelia Mary would be a neutral ship and there would be no anger, hatred, disagreements or arguing tolerated.

As they all agreed to this, it was already a little under twenty-four hours into the flight. The Earth was by now more than a million and a half miles away, and just a blue dot no bigger than the head of a pin.

They all soon adjusted to life aboard Amelia Mary, and soon the Earth and their lives on it were, not forgotten, but set aside, as important things came up on a regular daily basis on the Amelia requiring their constant attention.

Dr. Louis-Hart, the Science Officer, was making some observations out of one of the windows when he noticed a strange light. He said that it seemed to be keeping a safe distance from the ship and that it was also in a completely stationary location in space.

"What could that be," Capt. Young inquired, to which none of the crew could explain.

Louis-Hart immediately began taking notes and sketches of whatever it was. He saw that it was spherical, had two large "windows" for lack of a better word and a set of two solar arrays as well as a massive antenna that was pointed away from the ship. He estimated that it was more than sixty feet tall and spread out for more than one hundred feet.

Finally, young Lieutenant Kiselow, the chief engineer, came over and looked at the sketches and then out of the window. "Hello, girl," he said with a big smile on his boyish face. "How have you been?"

"You know her… it?" Captain Young asked.

"Yes, Captain," Kiselow said. "That is Inanna. She was sent out years ago to explore the Kuiper Belt. I worked on her briefly, and then she was launched."

"So, how the hell did she get here?" Louis-Hart asked.

"I have no idea," Kiselow replied. "The last I heard was that she was on her way back and, supposedly, she got hit by something that destroyed her… Well, at least that was the official report, but you know how accurate they are. Wow, what an opportunity to take her back home."

Everyone stopped what they were doing, trying to figure out what to say or do next. Finally, Lieutenant Kiselow asked a question that everyone should have guessed was coming, but no one did, except, of course, Amelie Mary's two well-trained captains.

"Captain, can we please …" he paused before continuing, but before he could do that, both captains replied in unison.

"No," they said. "We do not have the room to store anything that size aboard this ship."

Kiselow kept arguing that the Inanna should be recovered, but for every argument he gave, Captain Young and Captain Mombassa had one, and that was all they needed. They said…

"Because we said NO!" Naturally, that was supposed to be that, but unfortunately, Lieutenant Kiselow continued to argue.

The small ship was still there when everyone went to sleep… everyone except Kiselow, who was supposed to be watching the bridge to make sure nothing was wrong. Instead, he decided to spend his shift looking out the window at the Inanna. He managed to keep control for several hours before something snapped inside him.

He left his post and ran to the storage area, not walking. Once there, he stole an atmosphere suit and a booster pack. Once he got the equipment on, he went to one of the airlocks, opened the door, stepped in, and closed the door behind him.

As the air was drawn out of the airlock, there was a very slight drop in air pressure throughout the rest of the ship. The atmospheric pressure monitors measure to the closest .000001 atmospheres, either positive or negative, so when the pressure dropped beyond that, an alarm rang throughout the ship.

"Computer, what is going on," Captain Young yelled as she woke from a sound sleep.

"Airlock three has been depressurized," the computer replied.

"Who…," the captain asked.

"Lieutenant Kiselow, he is leaving the ship."

"What! … Oh no, no, he isn't!" Captain Young stated angrily. "Computer, lock all external hatches and do not open them, except when you receive an order from Captain Mombassa or me," Captain Young again ordered the computer to follow her orders as her anger intensified. "Do you understand?"

"Understood," the computer replied as the sound of hatches locking echoed throughout the ship. That sound was quickly joined by the sound of an airlock door opening, and Kiselow threw his helmet across the chamber and cussed so loudly that it was lucky the windows in the hull didn't shatter.

"Computer, I want that thing destroyed and Kiselow held in his quarters until we can get this straightened out," Captain Young angrily ordered as she stood at Kiselow's abandoned post on the bridge.

"Captain, please do not do this right now. We need the data Inanna holds!" Louis-Hart pleaded. We must download the data before Inanna is destroyed. As the Science Officer on board, it is my duty to insist that data is retrieved. It may hold imperative information that may one day save the Earth from destruction, and we need that data!"

Captain Young thought for a second before telling the crew, "Okay, we have ten minutes." They had only ten minutes to get the data, and Inanna would be destroyed. If there was going to be any argument, she would hit the button herself, and all of the data would be lost. The systems crew immediately flew into action and set about finding a way to link to Inanna's hard drive and retrieve the data.

"I've made the connection," Louis-Hart yelled from the ship's main computer. It took him eight minutes to make the connection, leaving only two minutes to retrieve more than a yottabyte of information. At the rate the transfer was being made, he would be lucky to be able to download more than one hundred terabytes or so in the remaining time; he walked to the bridge and begged the captain for more time. "Three hours should allow me to get it all," Louis-Hart said. Once again, the captain refused to listen.

In frustration, Louis-Hart decided to appeal to Captain Mombassa, but in support of her co-captain, she reluctantly refused to intervene.

Rushing back to the computer, Louis-Hart said he would keep downloading until Inanna could no longer transmit.

"Ready the port weapon," Captain Young said as she walked to the defense panel.

"Weapon ready, ma'am," the crewman in charge of the weapons said.

"Fire," she ordered in a commanding. "Did you hear me…? I said fire". The crewman sat staring at the computer screen with his hands in his lap. "I said fire," she shouted as her anger grew. Once again, the crewman ignored her order, but he backed away from the console this time. Immediately, Captain Young reached down and pulled a pistol from her belt. "Fire or I will kill you," she ordered as she put the gun to the crewman's head. "I swear if you don't fire right now, you will die!" Her eyes suddenly looked crazed, and it was apparent to all on the bridge that something within her had snapped; the Captain had lost all control.

"No," the terrified crewman replied, which made Captain Young even more furious and utterly out of control. She grabbed the crewman by his hair and dragged him toward the console as if to give him one last chance, but instead of doing what he was ordered to do, he fought back.

The fight only lasted a minute before Young once again placed the gun against the crewman's temple. This time, he knew that he was a dead man.

Captain Mombassa, Lieutenant Asianne, and everyone on the bridge saw what was going to happen, but no one could move; they had no time; they were terrified that Captain Young, in her fury, would instantly kill the crewman and then turn the gun on them! The tension mounted as another crewman came from below deck. He never said a word as he hid behind the door; he could see his commanding officer was shooting his best friend, so he also took out the gun from his belt, lowered his weapon, and fired directly at Captain Young. As the captain fell, the gun she was holding dropped to the floor and was immediately confiscated by Lieutenant Asianne.

A few seconds later, Captain Mombassa took charge. "Get Captain Young's body out of here," she ordered. "I don't care what you do with it, but I do NOT want it on the bridge!"

Two crewmen immediately rushed over and carried Captain Young's body out. Later, a couple of the crew who had witnessed the murder of Captain Samantha Young spread rumors that, after she had been shot, her body was taken and floated into space, but no one knew for sure, and if Captain Mombassa knew, she never said anything.

She no doubt thought that not knowing was better for ship morale than knowing, so she kept silent. Still, she and Captain Young had become close friends during the long training period for the mission, and she was utterly perplexed as to why such a terrible event could have occurred and why her friend had acted as she had done!

Finally, when things were somewhat calm, Captain Mombassa turned to Louis-Hart and told him he had one hour to gather as much information as possible.

"Thank you," Louis-Hart replied. "I am sure we will get everything that's there."

"Good," Captain Mombassa replied. "By the way… my name is Urula. I do not answer to Sir. Do you understand?"

"Yes, sir," Louis-Hart said. I am sorry. I understand, Captain Urula." He was smiling, nearly even laughing, despite all that had just occurred. Apparently, Captain Mombassa's relaxed handling of a bleak mutinous situation had already set the tone for the rest of the mission. After all, no charges could be laid until they were back on earth, time enough for all the accusations. Then, suddenly, everyone sighed, a sign of relief.

Captain Young's death was not forgotten; in a year, no doubt back on Earth, a significant fuss would be made and the crewman charged with disobeying an order, and the other with taking the life of a commanding officer, also naturally charges made against Lieutenant Kiselow for leaving his post, but for now all was back to semi-normal, and he was able to rejoin the crew.

Surprisingly, though, the command structure was still there. Everything somehow seemed more relaxed, more cordial, and more informal. The officers sat with crewmen for meals and poker games, and the tensions of the first few days disappeared. Of course, there were disagreements, but they never escalated, and if the captain thought they might… it was time for a boxing match in the cargo room.

The crew loved these matches. They were always held under strict rules, and things were never, ever allowed to get too far, but they did settle disputes and inner frustrations and also gave the crew some entertainment at the same time.

One match occurred between a female crew member from the galley and one of the men from engineering. It was all over the fact that he walked in the shower area while she was having a shower. She claimed that the young engineer paused a little too long looking at her before she was finally able to get him to leave. After the match, all was forgiven, and when they were off duty, they spent a lot of their downtime together.

One day, about a week after liftoff, the Captain decided to try something that no one had ever done before. With some help from the crew, she turned an old telescope someone brought on board at a ninety-degree angle from the actual galactic plane. It was amazing. There was just blackness, just this fantastic blackness, nothing but pitch black.

The crew was encouraged to keep a digital diary of their feelings and thoughts during the trip. One entry stuck out above all others. It reads, "It is so strange looking back and knowing that our planet is there, with billions of people living on it: beautiful forests, gardens, beaches, cliffs, and white clouds to please the senses. Now I look back, and there is nothing! The blue dot that was our home has long since disappeared. It is so lonely out here, even with all the people on board the Amelia Mary... It seems like a ghost ship; it is so strange for us to be so together, yet so much alone, hurtling through space."

Most of the crew and officers constantly felt this feeling of emptiness, but outside of the diaries, no one ever spoke of it.

According to Captain Mombassa, one good thing was that there was a recreational area that was naturally lit by the sun. The temperature was comfortable at 70 degrees, there was a soft breeze flowing through living plants, and there were even birds flying around singing and helping the crew relax.

One of the junior officers and Kiselow were down there a lot. The crew spread rumors that a love match was occurring between them, but they were in the middle of an argument over who could get the deepest tan before they returned to Earth. They were warned about getting skin cancer by Doctor Giovanni, but that didn't matter…they were there a couple of hours a day… every day, and they were both a deep bronze even after just a few days.

All in all, the trip so far has been uneventful, except for Captain Young's tragic death. The space satellite that had caused all the problems is now just a fading memory, but out of respect, Captain Mombassa ordered that Captain Young's name and any mention of the incident be forbidden.

The scanners also didn't report anything eventful until the ship was more than a month away from Earth… which was sadly starting to become a fading memory.

"Collision in two hours," the computer said coldly. "Evasion maneuver Sigma Alpha 3 recommended."

"I don't see anything," Louis-Hart yelled. "The screens are clear!"

"Nothing out of the forward port, Captain," an ensign yelled, confirming what Louis-Hart had said. Lieutenant Kiselow ran from window to window looking for something that the scanners may have found, but, just like with the others… there was nothing to see.

"Collision in one hour and fifty minutes," the computer announced again.

"I hate that damn thing," Kiselow said as he ran from window to window again. Once again, there was nothing to see. Then he turned back and looked at the scanner screen. A large mass of 150,000 kilometers was in front of the ship, and it was moving toward them. "There is something there," he yelled as he looked at the screen.

"What is it?" Captain Mombassa asked as she entered and moved to her seat on the bridge.

"I have no idea," Kiselow answered. He grabbed Louis-Hart and stood him in front of the scanner. "We should be able to see it. It is right in front of us."

"Collision in one hour forty-five minutes," the computer stated.

"Activate view screen," the captain immediately ordered. The screen lowered from the ceiling, and she could see what they were flying toward. There were no large asteroids as she had expected to see; instead, the space in front of them was slightly distorted and slightly lighter than the space behind it. "Computer, magnify the view screen 1,200 percent." She commanded. As soon as the image changed, Captain Mombassa saw millions of tiny, jagged spheres forming into one massive cloud.

"Collision in one hour and forty minutes," the computer stated. "Evasive maneuver recommended."

"Christ, how big is this thing?" Mombassa asked all the officers on the bridge.

"Captain, it is too big to go around," Louis-Hart replied as he looked at the forward scanner. "We are going to have to go through it. We have no choice."

"Maybe we can blow our way through," she said out loud, thinking of the defensive weapons the ship was carrying.

"Captain," the weapons officer answered. "I know the targets are small, but unfortunately, if we used the weapons, it would cause a chain reaction that could worsen the situation. I would strongly recommend not using the weapons at this time."

"Captain, the radiation from the cloud is at a dangerous level," Louis Hart stated. "Weapon Station is correct. If we fired into the target, a nuclear explosion would rival a burning sun. Everything within twenty astronomical units would be destroyed, creating major solar flares that might even destroy our Earth."

"Collision in one hour thirty minutes," the computer stated again. "Evasive action is recommended."

"No kidding," Captain Mombassa said sarcastically. Then she started to get irritated with the computer and asked. "Computer...what do you recommend we do?" The computer didn't have any suggestions, so the captain immediately ordered that the computer's voice be shut down. The order was followed up immediately, and the computer remained, even though everyone could still hear the collision warning it had given in their heads.

One could have heard a pin drop as Captain Mombassa looked across at the bridge crew. They were supposed to be the best, and now was their time to prove it. "I need an idea, and I need it now!" she stated quietly as she took a drink of coffee from a cup some crewman had placed by her chair.

For a few seconds, there was total silence. Apparently, no one had a suggestion. Then, one crewman in attendance got up the nerve to say something. He had no idea what the reaction was going to be, but he had a kind of stupid idea—at least it was an idea. "Captain," he started. I am from Kentucky, and we have a game we play on Saturday. It works almost every time."

"Well," Mombassa said. "Get it out!"

"Yes, Captain," he continued. "We take our truck and drive as fast as possible towards a deep mud pit." He saw a look of confusion spread around the bridge crew.

"Anyway, we go so fast that we don't sink into the mud; it just flows around our tires, and we go straight through it with no trouble." Then he explained that rocks can even be thrown some distance if the front of the truck hits them. "Captain, I suspect that just might work for us as well as it does for the trucks."

Captain Mombassa thought a minute, asked the crewman a few questions, and finally decided that since no one else had any ideas of what to do, and as the crewman's idea sounded a little logical, they would go for it. She immediately ordered the entire crew to use anything they could find to reinforce the forward sectors of the ship. It took about a half hour to shore up the hull. "I want everyone behind sector 33 immediately," Mombassa said into the intercom.

It only took about ten minutes for the crew to move to the ship's rear. All the bulkheads were sealed. Life support decreased for the front sectors and increased for the sectors where the crew hid. All shields were directed toward the bow, leaving the ship's rear unprotected.

"Computer set the engines," the captain ordered. "Sixty-minute burn, 110 percent power." Within a second, the computer screens showed the engines were at full power. They also showed that the collision was less than an hour away. "Computer, sixty-minute burn now!" The engines fired into action, and Captain Mombassa and the bridge crew were thrown back into their seats as the spaceship increased speed to as fast as the engines would allow Amelia Mary to go.

"Captain, we have exceeded maximum speed, and it is still increasing," Kiselow said as he tried to keep the ship on course. "Impact in five minutes," he reminded the crew.

"Brace for impact now," Captain Mombassa ordered her crew.

In the rear of the ship, more than a hundred crew members gathered as close together as humanly possible. The room echoed with the sounds of prayers in every religion and every conceivable language. In those potentially catastrophic minutes, differences in religion didn't matter. The crew was asking for help from any and every deity around, and even non-believers found themselves uttering a silent prayer.

"One minute before impact," Lieutenant Kiselow called out as everyone on the bridge braced for the inevitable.

"May God bless us all," Mombassa said as she strapped herself into her chair. "I think we are going to need Him."

"Thirty seconds," Kiselow said as the screen before him turned solid black.

The first impact came just a few seconds later. The ship was jolted hard on the port side. Some of the bridge crew were thrown to the floor, but most were fine. A couple had severe wounds, and their blood flowed onto the deck; again and again, the ship shook as one rock after another hit the hull. "Hull breach section four," Kiselow yelled. A second later, sections seven and nine lost pressure. "Seven and nine breached," Kiselow called out. "Atmosphere is leaking from all forward sections."

"Make sure the bulkheads hold," Captain Mombassa yelled back. Kiselow and another crewman sat at the computer scanning ahead, increasing the structural integrity of the hull and bulkheads. "How much longer do we have?"

"We should clear the field in less than three minutes if we continue at our current speed," Lieutenant Kiselow stated, knowing that those three minutes would be the longest any of them had ever lived.

"Can we last that long," Dr. Louis-Hart asked as he helped the medical officer, Dr. Giovanni, with the most seriously wounded.

"Hard to tell," Kiselow replied. "Let's pray so, she is taking a real shitty beating."

As soon as he said that, one of the giant rocks in the cloud smashed into the bow. The shutter shook the entire ship, and the bridge was filled with smoke within seconds. Captain Mombassa immediately ordered the bridge crew to do air masks. The luckiest were the wounded... they were located beneath the smoke and had no problem breathing, but even that was hard to say how long that would last. "How much longer," Captain Mombassa inquired.

"Two minutes," Kiselow yelled back. "Engines are at seventy percent. Shields are not doing much better." Immediately, Captain Mombassa ordered him to return the engines to one hundred percent. Lieutenant Kiselow said that there was nothing he could do. "Captain," he yelled. "We're lucky we have that much left. They have taken a beating... worse than us."

"Do the best you can," the captain said reassuringly. Inside, she felt like she was on the edge of a precipice, but she knew that if they were going to make it, she had to stay calm. "I have an idea," she said. Then she turned to Doctor Louis-Hart. "Divert all life support from the uninhabited sections to the bridge." Louis-Hart did as he was told. "Now, everyone hangs on," she called out as everyone grabbed onto consoles and seats. A couple of people caught the bulkhead.

  Once everyone was relatively safe, she ordered one of the crew members to count down from ten. Once the counter reached one, Captain Mombassa hit a button on her console. Suddenly, a roaring noise filled the bridge. Only then did the bridge crew realize that she was venting the atmosphere from the cabin to get the smoke out into space. One by one, the bridge crew began suffering from oxygen deprivation. It started with shaking, and two or three, including the cocky young chief engineer, passed out and fell to the floor. Mombassa also felt the effects as she

repeatedly hit the button to close the vent.
"Oxygen levels at ten percent," Dr Giovanni warned as she looked at a scanner she carried.

"All intact vents open to the maximum," Captain Mombassa ordered. The command was followed, and within a minute, oxygen levels were back to normal. Then, the damage reports began coming in. Captain Mombassa already knew the bow of the ship was badly damaged, but luckily, it wasn't damaged enough to be a risk to the crew.

"Captain," the navigator stated with intense relief. "We passed the last of the cloud. We are now in open space once again."

One could feel the bridge crew's elation and intensity of having survived. The captain thanked God, as did the rest of the bridge crew. Then, she issued the all-clear for the rest of the crew, stating that the ship was safe, but sections one through ten were off-limits until repairs could be completed.

Captain Mombassa then ordered a Class V3 probe to be launched into a stationary position more than a thousand kilometers into the field. "Has it transmitted a warning on all frequencies and in all languages and full strength? " she inquired. "Are we still on course?"

"Captain, I'm afraid we are now more than 1.5 million kilometers off course," the navigator replied. The captain looked at her briskly and ordered her to get the ship back on course. The navigator scanned her computer and fired the maneuvering thrusters for a five-second burn, and once that was complete, a three-minute burn would have taken them back to the location where they should have been less than four hours before.

"This is a warning from the Terran Space Expeditionary Council ship W.S.S. Amelia Mary," a voice said from the computer console. "This space area has been declared a danger to navigation. All ships plot a new course to avoid this hazard."

"Well, at least THAT is working," Captain Mombassa exclaimed with a slight smile. "Okay, fellows, let's get the repairs done. Let me know when we get back on course." Then, as her eyes started to close, she transferred command to Doctor Louis-Hart and went to her cabin to rest. Doctor Giovanni followed her to her cabin and, without knocking, walked in and sat down on the bed.

"Urula," Janet Giovanni started. "I have been a doctor for more than twenty years and your friend for longer. You did a hell of a job getting us through all this mess, but suddenly, I sense something is wrong. Are you okay?"

"Janet," Urula Mombassa replied. "I am just tired, I think. It has been a long day, and I slept poorly last night."

"Poppycock," Janet Giovanni replied with a laugh in her voice. "I remember times when we partied for a week without sleep, and you didn't need sleep for two days after that. You remember back when we were cadets." Doctor Giovanni was laughing as the memories flashed through her head. Captain Mombassa smiled and reminded Janet that it was long ago and that the two of them had aged a lot since then. "Urula, ten years is NOT a long time."

"Well, it is for me!" Captain Mombassa replied, realizing that maybe Janet was right; perhaps something was wrong. She had never felt suddenly so exhausted in her entire life, but as the sole Captain on the Amelia Mary, she wouldn't admit that even to her friend.

"Well, Urula, I want you to lay on the bed for a moment and let me check you out just to be safe," Doctor Giovanni said with a knowing smile. In fact, besides your reaction to all the recent drama, I think maybe I know why you may be feeling so very tired."

Captain Mombassa did as the doctor told her to. After all, though she hated to acknowledge it as captain, on a starship, the medical officer had even more authority than the ship's captain or a fleet admiral.

Doctor Giovanni took a small computer from her pocket. After a series of sweeps along the captain's body, she looked up from the screen and said, "Oh my God, Urula!" but it wasn't a frightened exclamation…it was more of a surprise.

"Janet, what is it," Captain Mombassa asked. She didn't know if she was frightened at what she was going to hear, or if she felt angry at the intrusion by her friend, but she was certainly curious about what Janet had to say. Unfortunately, her friend wasn't ready to give her the answer just yet.

After a few minutes, Doctor Giovanni took her by the hand as Captain Mombassa tried to sit up and get off the bed. "I don't think you should get up just yet," Janet commanded. "I have a few more tests to run before you get up." It took another hour and a couple of trips to the infirmary before Doctor Giovanni was ready to give the captain her diagnosis.

"It's about time," Captain Mombassa stated as her patience grew thinner and thinner.

"Urula," Giovanni began. "You are dehydrated, your iron is low, your blood sugar is abnormally high, and your hormones are off the chart."

"That's it?" Captain Mombassa asked with a shrug.

"Oh no… not in the least," Doctor Giovanni answered. It was hard for her to keep from laughing, but after catching the concerned look on her best friend's face puzzled face she was able to do so.

"Urula, while you were back on Earth, you picked up a parasite still with you."

"That's not possible," Captain Mombassa declared forcefully. "I was scanned several times before I boarded the ship and they didn't pick anything, so how could I have a parasite?"

"My friend, take my word for it… you have a parasite, and it isn't one the scanners would have recognized," Doctor Giovanni explained.

"I didn't go anywhere where I could get a parasite," Captain Mombassa replied. "I swear to God that I didn't!" By now Captain Mombassa's voice was full of anger and fear but the worse she got the more Doctor Giovanni started laughing. Finally, her friend stopped laughing; at least laughing loudly and decided to tell her friend Urula what the parasite really was.

"Urula," she said as she took the captain by the hand and sat her down in a chair. "My dear friend, you are pregnant, and I am guessing that you are about four months on."

"What?" "Don't be ridiculous Janet!" Then she looked into her friend's eyes and realized Janet was dead serious. "How, oh my God, how did THAT happen," Captain Mombassa asked rhetorically. Doctor Giovanni was still having fun with it, so she gave Captain Mombassa a quick lesson on the birds and bees! Something which the captain at that moment really did not appreciate.

"Janet, I swear, I only had sex once a couple of months before we left, and that, believe me, was protected sex, so I don't see how?"

"Hey, it happens," Doctor Giovanni said before she suggested ways to keep the "problem" under control, each of which Captain Mombassa rejected without a thought.

It was no more than ten seconds before the intercom came alive. "Doctor Giovanni, please report to the infirmary immediately," it said. It repeated the message a couple of times before Giovanni got up to leave, but, for some reason, she insisted that Captain Mombassa follow her.

Once they reached the infirmary, Dr. Giovanni was confronted with more than a dozen women who were on sick call, precisely for the same symptoms Captain Mombassa was suffering from.

A quick scan, a couple of tests, and the diagnosis shocked Doctor Giovanni much more than even discovering that her best friend, the captain, was with her child. It turned out that every woman sitting in the waiting room was pregnant. Most admitted that they had sex a couple of times before they left the earth, but there were a couple who said they were still virgins.

Naturally, Doctor Giovanni didn't exactly trust their statements of celibacy; as the mystified captain returned to her cabin to wait for the results, the Doctor conducted a quick internal exam, which confirmed that these women were virgins and they were indeed pregnant.

While the astounded Doctor Giovanni examined each of the women, more and more of the female crew walked into the room... each one was pregnant, and each was about four months pregnant.

A test run on each of the women revealed something even stranger than all the women appearing to be pregnant: all the fetuses had the same paternal DNA. Even though Giovanni didn't believe it possible, the clinical facts were staring her in the face, so immediately, she began questioning each of the women.

Because of the questions, Doctor Giovanni was able to get a description of a man whom all the women had known during their last leave on Earth. True, each woman had a different name for him, but the descriptions were all the same.

The captain returned to her cabin and had just laid her head down on the pillow for about five minutes when the call came. "Captain, could you please report to the infirmary?" Giovanni asked. The captain opened her half-closed eyes and immediately responded to the message. Within a few minutes, she was fully dressed and headed straight back to the infirmary.

"What is it now," Captain Mombassa asked, but before the doctor could answer, the captain added, "This had better be good!"

"Oh, it is," Giovanni said, but she wasn't smiling this time. Before she said another word, she took the captain by the hand, led her to a chair, and ordered her to sit down. Captain Mombassa sat down nervously since she had no idea what the doctor would say.

"Janet, what is it?" the captain asked.

"Well, I don't know how to say this," Doctor Giovanni started. "You know we have twenty-six women on board," Mombassa said that was correct. Giovanni paused momentarily as she thought about what she would say next... or how she would say it. Finally, she decided that just saying would be the best way. "I have something strange to tell you…" Once again, she paused. "… Well, every woman on board the Amelia Mary is pregnant, and every one of them is due just about the same time you are due."

"Okay," Captain Mombassa said in total confusion.

"That isn't the strangest thing, though," Doctor Giovanni told her friend. The captain was almost too afraid to ask what any stranger could be, but she did anyway, and the answer shocked her. "Urula, every baby… including yours… has the same father."

"What!" Captain Mombassa asked as if she didn't quite understand her friend's statement.

"The babies all have the same father." Naturally, Doctor Giovanni couldn't explain how this could have happened, especially since a few of the women were virgins before the launch and were still virgins.

"Who is the father?" The captain asked as the fog finally left her thoughts.

"I don't have a name," Giovanni answered. She explained that each woman had a different name for the man, but they all had the same description. I had the computer come up with a picture." The doctor walked over, hit a couple of buttons on the computer console, and immediately, the man's picture appeared on the screen.

Captain Mombassa's eyes brightened as she looked at the screen. "I know him," she said. She stared closer at the picture. "Yeah, I remember him. He was standing in the entryway to the residency training pods we lived in the last three months before the launch. He seemed to know everybody and made it a definite point to shake everyone's hand to wish them luck on the journey. I had never seen him before, and I didn't think he was supposed to be there, but said nothing as he did have the proper ID on him."

"You know, I now remember him too," Doctor Giovanni stated. "He was there at the doorway the whole time. Strangely enough, I didn't want to touch him because I had no idea who the hell he was. "Yeah, come to think of it," Captain Mombassa said. "I also remember that. Tell me, Janet, how in the world does a casual handshake get someone pregnant?"

"You know now I remember, I actually felt something as he shook my hand, like the tip of a pin, poke lightly into my hand, when I shook his hand," Mombassa said. "But it was so slight; I thought I was being silly. Janet, I don't know how, but that must have been how he did it." Then Captain Mombassa thought for a moment. Her eyes went blank as she called on the computer to answer several questions. "Computer," she finally said. "How long has it been since launch, and how much longer do we have until we find Earth 2?"

"It has been thirty-two days since we launched," the computer responded. Time until Earth 2 landing ... four months and twenty-eight days." The two friends didn't say a word to each other, but they both realized the same thing at the same time... all the babies were going to be born very close to the day that the Amelia Mary would touch down on the planet... that is if the Twin Earth planet even existed.

"Computer, can we contact Earth?" The captain enquired.

"Earth is currently behind the solar horizon and may not be contacted at this time," the computer responded.

"Damn," Mombassa yelled. "How could this have happened to us? We had all security we could, and there were so many scans, I thought I would start glowing from them." She was fit to be tied at that moment and suffering from command stress and also extreme hormonal changes; Doctor Giovanni especially realized this when a tray full of beakers went flying across the room and smashed against the wall. A quick injection from the doctor calmed the pregnant Captain's nerves to a point where she could be once again spoken to.

"Urula," Janet Giovanni stated firmly. "Come on now, girl, take it easy. There isn't anything we can do about it now. We will have to wait to see how things go, but I am sure everything will be fine!"

Captain Mombassa didn't have time to say or do anything else. The injection kicked in, and she became so relaxed that Doctor Giovanni ordered her back to her cabin to rest. Then, she turned her attention to the other women in the room.

Back on the bridge, the linguistics officer, Lieutenant Asianne, scanned frequencies to see if anything was in the space around them. He had been sitting in the same position for more than six hours when a message came in. It was on a rarely used frequency… at least seldom used by the World Space Agency, but there was something there. It was weak and full of static, but there was still something coming from behind them. "Asianne, focus on that transmission," Louis-

Hart ordered. "I want to know what it is saying."

"I am doing my best," Lieutenant Asianne replied as he changed more and more settings.

"Can you tell me where it is coming from?" Louis Hart asked.

"Sir, all I can tell you is that it is coming from an approximate location of Mars," he replied. Lieutenant Asianne had served hundreds of missions throughout the solar system and was adept at using his tools and making them work. "Yes, sir, the transmission comes from an object orbiting Mars."

"What is it," Louis-Hart asked.

"It is a radio transmission, and it is transmitted on a frequency of 44.8 megahertz," Asianne stated with a puzzled tone. "We have not used that frequency in more than thirty years." Suddenly, Asianne stood up. He could not believe his ears as the message came through.

"W.S.S. Amelia Mary, this is Earth calling... can you hear me," a voice said through the crackle of the static. "W.S.S. Amelia Mary, this is Earth calling... can you hear me?" It was someone who was sending out a signal to a ship they knew was out there somewhere and hoping for a response. Asianne remembered doing the same thing when she was a girl in Vanuatu. Manu spent nights in her room talking to the crew of the International Space Station, and she knew how the person on the other end of that transmission must have felt.

"This is the Amelia Mary," Asianne replied. "We can hear you?" While Lieutenant Asianne was straining to hear what was being said, Louis-Hart ordered that the captain was to be brought to the bridge. Unfortunately, the Captain was in no condition to go to the bridge… a fact that Dr. Giovanni was more than eager to relay.

"Amelia Mary… my name is Chriss Santos, I picked up one of your signals are you there" the voice asked.

"Yes, yes… Chriss, this is Lieutenant Asianne of the Amelia Mary," Asianne replied. "Where are you located?" Now, because of the distance the signal had to travel it was taking more than a few minutes between messages… time the crew used searching the computers on board to find out what was going on and who Chriss Santos was.

"Lieutenant Asianne," Chriss explained. "I live in Eureka, Oregon."

That gave the crew enough information to go on. A quick check of the computer showed that Chriss Santos was a fifteen-year-old boy who was a freshman at Eureka High School. He was a computer science major who had won several awards for work he had done in communication technology.

"Chriss, can you hear me," Asianne asked as Giovanni stepped through the door. "We have a situation on board, and we need your help."

"I will do what I can," Chriss answered as Asianne handed the microphone control over to Doctor Giovanni.

"Chriss, my name is Doctor Janet Giovanni. Please write this down carefully," Giovanni said. "I am going to start with an authentication code... ready?"

"Yes, ma'am," Chriss replied.

"WSS489IJ6," Giovanni said, "Did you get that?" Once Chriss read it back to her, Giovanni gave him the message. "The Amelia Mary badly damaged all female officers and crew assaulted before launch and are all currently pregnant. We are now trying to develop a plan to handle the situation."

"Hurry up," the navigator yelled.

"Did you get that?" Giovanni asked, only to receive a static reply. "Did you get that?" Once again, she received no response.

"Damn, we lost him," Lieutenant Asianne said as he put his head on the console in total annoyance. Then, the doctor asked the only question that could be asked at a time like that… Asianne, did the message get through? "Janet, I have no idea. The signal cut out too fast to know one way or the other, and now, if we do not hear from Chris again, it will take us ten months to find out if the WSA got our message," replied the extremely frustrated Lieutenant.

"Well, make sure that the messages are archived, and the captain receives a copy when I let her back on duty," Doctor Giovanni stated. "Lieutenant Kiselow confirmed that the conversation was recorded and stored in the computer's auxiliary hard drive. Janet Giovanni acknowledged Kiselow and asked, "What else can happen?" By now, she was frustrated and extremely perplexed about what to do. After all, she was the only medical officer and had a spaceship filled with pregnant women, including the Captain of the Twin World Exploratory Operation. "Oh dear, I repeat, what more could happen!"

Now, anyone who has ever traveled anywhere knows that that is the one question you never, ever ask because, as on earth, night follows day, something will happen shortly afterward.

It was just seven days later when it happened... a once in a lifetime event. The Sun, Mercury, and Venus were in perfect alignment. By this time, Captain Mombassa, had decided to ignore the doctor's advice and return to duty and was back on the bridge when the light from outside the window faded. It wasn't much, but it was enough to be noticeable. The computer's voice came loudly. "Increased electromagnetic field detected. Take precautions!"

"Look at this," a crewman yelled from his station. He was looking out of a window and saw Venus and Mercury align. Then he saw something else. A huge solar flare exploded into space. According to his observations, the flare extended far beyond the orbit of Mercury and was traveling toward them at nearly the speed of light. The captain rushed toward the window and saw exactly why the crewman was so excited, for lack of a better word.

"Computers analyze," Captain Mombassa yelled.

"Solar radiation at fifty-seven percent of what the shields can hold," warned the computer. "Magnetic radiation one hundred thirty-three percent over the shield's capacity."

Captain Mombassa thought for less than a minute before she turned to Louis-Hart and Kiselow. "Where on the ship is the area where a magnetic strike would do the least damage," she asked. Louis Hart and Kiselow spoke momentarily, and Lieutenant Kiselow immediately got onto the intercom. "All crew and maintenance personnel, please hurry. Be aware that the Amelia Mary is heading for a collision with a massive solar flare five minutes from now."

"Captain, I'm sorry, but all repairs are not yet completed on the areas of the ship that were severely damaged," the ordinarily optimistic Kiselow started frantically.

"Kevin, are you okay? There is no crew there!" Louis-Hart responded. "All of the maintenance work in that area at the moment is being done by our ship's robots."

"Lieutenant, turn the ship," Captain Mombassa immediately ordered. "Place the damaged sections of the ship to face the sun," She looked for just a moment as if she was going to relax, but she wasn't going to in the least. "I would much rather lose some robots than one crew member."

The following five minutes were a flurry of activity all over the ship. Every hard drive from every computer and console was pulled and placed into safe areas. The patients in the infirmary were moved to places deep inside the ship, and titanium shields were lowered over every window, especially the windows on the bridge.

Turning the ship was a slow move. All maneuvering thrusters on the post side eventually fired, and as they did, the sun gradually moved into a location no longer visible from the bridge.

When the magnetic radiation hit the Amelia Mary, there was no impact and no other signs except that every light aboard the ship brightened and then turned off. That started in the areas next to the damaged sections and continued until it hit the bridge.

Because of extra shielding, it took longer for the effects to be noticed, but they did happen, and when they did, the bridge crew found themselves in total darkness.

"Is everyone alright?" Captain Mombassa asked. One by one, the bridge crew reported that they were all there and in good shape. "Section leaders report," Mombassa said into the intercom. She repeated it several times before an ensign told her that communications were down.

"Communications isn't the only system down, captain," Kiselow said as he looked at the only console operating. It was one of the design ideas Captain Young insisted on before the flight. The systems console on the bridge was to have a heavily shielded power supply of its own for just such situations.

"What else," Mombassa asked.

"Captain, power is down ship-wide," Kiselow said. "Life support is operating at twenty-five percent, engines and shields are down, and artificial gravity is operating at less than thirty-three percent."

"Captain…" that ensign started,"… there is one good piece of information."

"What's that," Mombassa asked.

"Captain, we are still on course and at our proper speed," the ensign said. "Four months, three weeks from Earth 2."

Captain Mombassa smiled at that news, but she already knew what she had to do. The problem was that with communications down, she could not talk to the crew, so she picked two of the lower-ranking bridge crew and ordered them to deliver a message to every member of the crew. The message said, "All crew members are to restrict talking and other activities aboard the ship. Each section must send ONE representative to the bridge to report damages and injuries."

Within minutes, reports began coming in. All sectors were safe, except for the ones damaged earlier, and there were no casualties. All computer hard drives had been replaced, and the computers rebooted. It was as if nothing had happened to the ship.

"Captain, all systems except life support are online," Kiselow said as he looked at his computer screen. "It is still operating at seventy-five percent."

"Are all communications up?" Mombassa asked to reconfirm what he had said. When he confirmed that communications were online, the captain opened a ship-wide channel and informed the crew of the ship's status. "To all officers and crew, this is your captain speaking. Thankfully, Amelia Mary is operating, and all systems, unfortunately, except life support, are working at one hundred percent capacity. To ensure we have no medical problems, we will all crew to curtail unnecessary talking, repair work, and all recreational activities. We are in no danger, but these procedures must be followed; in this situation, we need all the oxygen possible to survive."

A new junior officer, Ensign Italio Ricard, who had just graduated from the academy and was on his first flight, heard the news and started to tremble and shake. He was scared stiff and immediately started to panic after hearing the captain's announcement.

Even though his family had a long history of bravery in action, ranging from World War 2, through the Yellowstone eruption, to the Lunar Defense of 2089, young Italio unfortunately did not share that gene with his ancestors. "What are we going do?" he suddenly screamed as he went ballistic and frantically grabbed at a weapon that had fallen out of its holder on the wall. He then pointed the gun hysterically at anyone who came toward him. "We are all going to die!" The young engineer screamed out; his fear turned into full-blown panic.

"We are NOT going to die," another young officer firmly stated as she tried to get closer to him. "We will be alright as long as you calm down."

"Keep away, keep away!" he shouted at her. "No, we are going to die... we are all going to die," Ricard screamed. His voice was now a mixture of panic and crying, so it was hard to understand.

"Italio," the young officer said. "Think of how large this ship is." Ricard took a second and thought. "Don't you think they have redundant systems for everything on this ship and redundant systems to cover the redundant systems?"

"I guess so," he cried out, yet there was still fear in his voice, and he was by then crying his eyes out and waving the weapon at the young officer. Before he could say another word, his body suddenly stiffened, and then blue electrical charges surrounded his body. As he fell, the engineering crew observed one of the ship's security officers standing in the bulkhead.

The security officer ordered, "Restrain him immediately and get him to the infirmary. " Then he disappeared down the walkway.

It seemed that the communication line between the bridge and engineering had been accidentally left open, and the bridge crew had heard everything. On hearing what was going on, Captain Mombassa ordered the man to be subdued, restrained, and placed in a stasis tube until the situation with life support systems could be resolved.

Within minutes, one report after another came into the bridge of crewmen who had lost control of their emotions. Doctor Giovanni immediately realized that it may have been from a lack of oxygen or the stress of the last 15 minutes that caused them to break, but either way, it was not their fault. The captain and the command staff discussed the situation and all possible options until a decision was made.

Once again, the speakers came alive. "We just had a situation where someone was unable to control themselves and started panicking," the captain said. "Such behavior cannot be tolerated. Anyone who believes they cannot handle our current situation is ordered to proceed to the stasis tubes until repairs to the ship are completed." Within the hour, twelve men and women either were picked up or volunteered to enter the tubes.

"Captain...," the computer began. "...Oxygen levels are at fifty-three percent."

"Computer run a level three diagnostic on all ships systems," Mombassa commanded.

"Scan will take three hours and twenty-four minutes," the computer replied.

"How can we shorten that?" Mombassa asked the bridge crew. Lieutenant Kiselow was the first to speak up, but as was the ship's protocol, he didn't speak to the captain at that moment.

Instead, he spoke to the computer. "Computer, this is Lieutenant Kevin Kiselow," Kiselow began. "Authorization number 4467a," the computer recognized the authorization number and Kiselow as the chief engineer.

"Lieutenant Kiselow, what may I do for you," the computer asked.

"I have taken command on the Amelia Mary," Kiselow said. "I order you to ignore all previous commands issued to you within the last thirty minutes."

"All commands from Captain Mombassa have been deleted," the computer replied.

"Computer," Kiselow began. "Run a level three diagnostic on all systems related to life support on the ship."

At that moment, Captain Mombassa had no problem with Kiselow taking command, knowing he was right to do so, as all their lives depended on it.

Since Kiselow had taken command of the ship, his official title was captain, so when the computer responded a few seconds later, it was aimed at Kiselow instead of Captain Mombassa.

"Captain...," the computer said, "... the exhaust vents leading from the forward sections of the ship are blocked and are putting toxic gasses back into the ship's atmosphere," Kiselow asked the computer where the blockage was located. "Section seven, deck four," the computer responded. Then it added that it was in a service port near cabin five." Kiselow asked about the laptop, and it replied that the location was correct.

"That is awful close to the breach," Mombassa said. "Maybe too close!" Then she asked the computer what the conditions were in that location.

"Life support is within the parameters set for safe human existence," it replied.

Lieutenant Kiselow didn't wait more than a minute before returning command of the ship to Captain Mombassa. He then ordered some of his best people to meet him at the location of the blockage, left the bridge, and started running.

It took very little time for Kiselow and his people to reach the blockage. The area was full of fumes, but luckily, they were not strong enough to interfere with their mission. What they saw was a problem. A large asteroid was blocking the vent, which itself needed major repair.

As Kiselow looked around, he noticed something that shocked but didn't surprise him. There was a large hole where the asteroid had entered the ship, which had to be sealed before the blockage could be removed.

Once he reported that to the bridge, Captain Mombassa had only one thing to do. She ordered all of the crew, except the engineering crew and all officers besides Kiselow and herself, into the stasis tubes. At least that would keep them alive until the atmosphere throughout the ship could be returned.

"You all get into survival suits," Kiselow ordered his crew as he started down the hallway. He knew what had to be done, and he knew that he was the one who had to do it. He had to go and fix the hole from the outside. There was one thing Kiselow was sure of: He knew that his crew was loyal and would do their jobs no matter what, so he left them without a second thought as he continued to run down the hall.

It took a full fifteen minutes for Kiselow to get suited up and out through the airlock. By then, he had also gone to engineering and grabbed a sheet of argonlunium. It was light and flexible, but once it was treated with a spray that he had also grabbed, it was more potent than the material the ship was made of.

Although his crew could not see him, they could hear him attach himself to the hull. They also had radio communication, so they knew what he was doing and what he wanted them to do. His first order was for them to tie a lifeline to themselves as the air pressure was going to drop fast, and anything in that hallway was sure to be sucked into space. "All safely secured," was the message Kiselow received a few seconds later.

Lieutenant Kiselow began a countdown from ten. The crew knew that when he reached zero, their job was to pull the asteroid away from the hull as soon as they could, so when he hit zero, they did exactly what he wanted.

The asteroid moved slowly, and Kiselow could feel and see the air rushing out of the ship. Finally, the rock fell to the floor, and Kiselow slapped the argonlunium sheet onto the hull. It performed exactly as it should have. He bolted it down and sealed it tightly onto the hull. Then he sprayed the metal and watched as it turned from a soft plastic-like surface to a sheet of metal that was even stronger than the rest of the ship's body.

Then Kiselow ordered his people to make any repairs they had to do to the filter.

At the time, they had no idea how bad the damage was, but once they saw it, they were pleasantly surprised. There was a crack just before the filter compartment. It was about twenty feet long and easily fixed, and it was repaired by the time Kiselow got back into the airlock and back to his crew. He thought a minute before he asked the computer what the conditions were throughout the ship.

"Life support is returning to normal levels," the computer replied. "Oxygen at safe levels for human existence."

"Well, that's good," Kiselow said, echoed by the rest of his crew.

The ship sounded strange. There was total quiet except for the sounds of the engines. Kiselow and his crew walked through the hallways. Not one of them said a word, but Kiselow was thinking, with all the pregnancy problems aboard the Amelia Mary, maybe it would be a good idea for everyone to make the rest of the trip in statistics, and that was what he decided to do.

He and his crew changed into suits designed for the stasis tubes, and one by one, they stepped in and went to sleep. To get her to agree, he then advised the captain, due to her pregnancy, to also go into the stasis state while all life support systems fully recovered. She did not argue; she thought going into stasis for at least a few hours was a good idea as it would calm everyone down. Lieutenant Kiselow was the last one to go into his stasis tube. Before the door closed on his chamber, he said, "Computer, open all stasis tubes on June 15, 2174, at 8:30 AM... officers first and the crew one hour later." The computer confirmed the order, closed the door to Kiselow's tube, and put him to sleep for the rest of the trip.

As soon as the last tube closed, the computer reduced life support to nearly nonexistent, artificial gravity dropped to a mere three percent, and lighting was turned off. Only the systems vital to ship operations, even those running on minimum power, were left on.

At 8:00 on the date ordered, the computer began reactivating systems individually, starting with life support, gravity, and lighting. Other systems, in turn, also began performing at normal levels.

Half an hour after the systems began, the first stasis tubes opened, starting with Captain Mombassa and then the other officers. As soon as her mind cleared and she was able to think, her first question was how long they had been in stasis. "Captain," the computer began. You have been in stasis for over four and a half months."

"What! Who damn well ordered that?" Captain Mombassa demanded to know.

'Lieutenant Kiselow ordered all crew members to be placed in stasis and revived on this date and at this time," the computer replied.

Captain Mombassa looked at Kiselow's tube and saw that he was still in stasis. "Computer," she started. Can you hear me clearly?" Once the computer told her it could listen to her, she continued: "Computer, you are to keep Lieutenant Kevin Kiselow in stasis until seven days after we leave orbit around Earth 2. Do you understand?"

As the computer acknowledged her order, the captain started the process of getting her body back to normal. As she did, Dr. Giovanni came up to her.

"You can't do that," Giovanni said. "Urula, you know that is just wrong."

"Janet, you more than anyone should know why I HAVE to keep him in stasis," Captain Mombassa replied. "He has broken every rule in the book; think of all we missed while asleep. There could have been something that could have given us information, changed our understanding of the cosmos, possibly revealed things we could not imagine, and even ended all the pain and disease on Earth, and we missed it."

"I know, but...," Giovanni started.

"But what?" Captain Mombassa responded with a touch of anger in her voice. We ARE explorers and scientists." Her friend knew the captain, but when she made up her mind, nothing would change it. So, the doctor didn't say anything.

"Janet, wouldn't you have loved to have discovered an unknown planet and upon it found some kind of strange form of life and, from its analysis, have been the woman who found the cure for cancer?"

"Kiselow just didn't think… that's all it was," Doctor Giovanni replied, feeling very sorry for Lieutenant Kiselow; after all, he had saved all their lives.

"Well, I don't think he thought enough about our mission, Janet. I'm sorry, but I do not want him to see anything we find when we get to Earth 2. He'll wake up after we leave, and that is that."

With those words, the discussion ended, and the doctor commenced once again, examining each crew member as they exited their tubes.

"Planet detected," the computer said. "Distance 564,000 miles"

Captain Mombassa was extremely surprised by the announcement. She thought they had more time to prepare, but... this would change everything.

"Hmm, Urula," the doctor began. "Have a look at the crew." The captain looked but didn't notice anything special about them. "Urula, don't you see," she said. "All pregnancies look as if they are full term... even yours." The Doctor ran a scanner from a nearby console across the captain's swollen belly. "My friend," the doctor said. "I give you, oh, let's say another week, and this ship's population will increase by at least fifty percent.

The captain looked at all the female crew members and saw that they were all in the same state as she was, but although she was curious, Mombassa had other things to worry about. "Computer," Captain Mombassa said. "Give me all the data on the planet we are headed to."

The computer immediately replied, "It is a class one planet with an oxygen-nitrogen atmosphere, seventy percent water, seven continents, and polar caps made of water ice. Scans show a population of six billion humanoid creatures, most of which live in population centers. Scans also show one moon on a fixed orbit around the planet."

"Well, that sounds like a bag of possibilities," Doctor Giovanni said as she took a few seconds from her medical scans.

"What is their technological status," Mombassa asked.

"Scans show nuclear capability, current fossil fuel usage at eighty-five percent; they have the capability for air and limited space travel."

"Defense capabilities," Captain Mombassa asked as her final question.

"No defenses above the atmosphere," the computer replied. "Aerial defenses are limited to missiles, and ground defenses are also limited."

The bridge crew stopped working on those who were the last to be revived and rushed to the bridge. They could see a bluish-green dot as they looked out of the forward windows. It was about the size of the nail on the smallest of a woman's fingernails. "Time until orbit," Captain Mombassa asked.

"Seven days, four hours, and seventeen minutes until planetary orbit," the navigator replied.

"Are we picking up any transmissions from the planet's surface," was the captain's next question.

"Captain, transmissions from the planet are barely detectable," the communications officer replied. "I doubt they have the technology to broadcast this far into space." The captain ordered all frequencies to be scanned at all times and that she be informed the instant a readable signal is detected. Then, her attention turned back to the planet itself.

"Henry, does the planet have any artificial satellites," she asked.

"Captain," Louis-Hart replied. "Scans are showing that the planet has nearly ten thousand artificial satellites in various orbits around the planet," Mombassa asked their purpose. "Defense, communications, scientific experimentation and observation out into space."

"Well, that sounds familiar... doesn't it," Mombassa asked, referring to Earth's many space programs and the satellites they had launched into orbit. "I think we may have a few more than that, but I am unsure."

"Well," Louis-Hart stated. "I have a feeling that if Kiselow were here, he would know the Earth's exact satellite count."

"I am sure of that," Mombassa replied. "I have a feeling that he will regret missing all of this when he finally wakes up." The captain laughed, but only just a little. She didn't want to appear too pleased with what she had done. Still, every time she thought about letting Kiselow out of his stasis mode, she immediately became infuriated once again as the thoughts of what they might have missed rushed into her mind, and she knew that she was doing the right thing by keeping him out of it.

It had been quite a while since the crew of the Amelia Mary had been able to sit down and have a decent full meal, so, on the captain's orders, all sections were set on automatic, and every man and woman aboard the ship were ordered to the mess for a dinner of roast turkey, rye bread stuffing, vegetables, sautéed fruits, and deep-dish apple pie smothered with whipped cream for dessert. Usually, food was limited, but because of the celebration, those eating were allowed seconds and even thirds...a first for the ship.

Once everyone had eaten, they were allowed to relax. Some watched movies they had downloaded onto their computers before leaving Earth. Others lounged near oversized windows on the ship's bow, and others returned to their rooms and passed out onto their beds. Captain Mombassa was proud of her crew and was happy to give them their time because she knew the next few days would be more stressful than anything they had ever experienced.

    The captain spent the next few days making a detailed record of everything that had happened to the ship and crew over the past six months. She made it a particular point to write a report that the crew had unwillingly placed into stasis. The last thing she wrote was that Lieutenant Kevin Kiselow was deemed untrustworthy, and she added her recommendation that he be removed from duty and charged with sabotage. She knew that once the planet was explored, she might change her mind and erase her recommendation, but she would have to see.

The rest of the officers and crew were preparing the ship for landing and exploration, but a few took the time to write their thoughts about discovering a twin to planet Earth. Some writings were poetic, others were fiction, and others were scientific papers. No matter what was written or who had written it, the people of Earth would know precisely what the crew of Amelia Mary felt while they were at the dawn of discovery.

The communications officer's ears suddenly perked up when the ship was still a couple of days from the planet. "Captain, report to the bridge immediately," he said into the intercom.

Only a minute or two before, Mombassa and Asianne rushed through the door and took their positions on the bridge. "What is so important," Mombassa asked.

"Listen," the communications officer replied as he pushed a button on his console.

It was cracking badly, but it could be understood. "Our leaders will be meeting today to discuss genetic research currently being performed in the Dungrey Provence," a female voice said.

"Is that…," Mombassa started to ask.

"Yes," Asianne answered without waiting for her to finish. She turned to the communications console and asked the officer, "Are you running the transmission through the computer translator?" The answer was no. "Captain, whoever that is…they are speaking English."

"Captain, I am picking up other transmissions from the planet," the officer said. He played a little piece of each transmission. Most of them were in English, but some sounded as if they were in other Earth languages. Neither Mombassa nor Asianne could understand how what they were hearing could be possible.

"Where are those transmissions originating," Asianne asked.

"It is coming from the population centers on the planet's surface," the officer replied. He pointed at a screen at the front of the bridge. He had moved a scanner view screen so the captain could see what he was seeing. He was right…all the transmissions were coming from many points on the surface.

"This is very strange," Asianne said excitedly. It should not be happening." Captain

Mombassa agreed, and she ordered more scans and a detailed report of all the transmissions. Because of the number of languages, Asians would be very busy for a long time with no help.

Captain Mombassa just sat in her chair, looking out of the windows. The approaching planet was so beautiful and much like Earth that it made her think of home. *How could I have taken this mission*, she thought as her mind wandered back to her husband and daughter, whom she hadn't seen in so long. *Jenni's two now. I missed her birthday. I missed her opening her presents and blowing out the candles on her cake. How could I have ever left her?* The thoughts were sad and depressing, but she kept her mind on her job even if her heart was millions of miles away.

"Captain...," one of the bridge crew started. "... There has been a launch from the planet." Mombassa looked at her screen as her senses came back to the present. She believed they were still well beyond the planet's defensive weapons, so she wasn't nervous. "The launch took place at a civilian facility. I cannot see any defensive technology in the immediate area."

She knew they were just beyond the orbit of the planet's moon, so she ordered that the ship be placed in a stationary orbit 100,000 miles from its surface. Put us directly between the earth and its moon," she said. "I don't want them to know we're here until we know more about them."

It took the ship a day and a half to be placed in its final position, but it was not going to be unnoticed for long. Within two hours after the Amelia Mary took the position, Louis-Hart saw that the ship they had seen launched earlier had broken orbit and was moving toward them. He was the intercom and told the captain she should be getting ready since they would expect visitors shortly.

"Maintain scans on that ship," she said as she stepped onto the bridge. "I want to know what we are facing." Then she ordered the view screen lowered and an extreme shot of the ship. From what she could see, it wasn't anything special... in fact, it reminded her of the shuttles the United States used in the latter twentieth century.

"Captain," Louis-Hart said. "The ship has a crew of nine humans, six men and three women. The atmosphere is nitrogen/oxygen, and scans do NOT detect any weaponry built into the ship or if the crew is carrying anything dangerous." Then, he noticed something extraordinary about the ship. Its flight lights were flashing—first two flashes, then three flashes, then five, and finally seven before the sequence repeated itself. "I know what that is," he said.

"Well," Mombassa asked.

"The simplest form of communication is mathematics," he said.

"So," she said.

"They are sending us prime numbers between one and ten," he said with a big grin. "That's a sign that they are an intelligent species."

Captain Mombassa acknowledged that and ordered the following response. "Flash the lights in the following sequence…one, four, six, eight, and nine," she ordered. "Continue until we get a response." The response was not extended in coming. The lights on the ship came on and stayed on as it got closer and closer.

"Unidentified ship," the radio said with the first message in a while. "This is the Shuttle Epsilon. Can you hear us?"

"Shuttle Epsilon, this is the W.S.S. Amelia Mary of Earth," Mombassa said.

"W.S.S. Amelia Mary," the voice continued. "Please allow us passage aboard your ship to talk and learn about each other."

Mombassa was concerned but decided to allow the smaller ship's crew aboard...after all, her crew had all of the weapons, so they were safe. "I am going to dock them at the stern," she said. "I don't think they will try anything, but I don't want them on the bridge that soon anyway. The rest of the bridge crew agreed, and docking instructions were transmitted to the Epsilon while Mombassa was ready for the visitors. Then, Mombassa ordered that the ship be placed on station keeping, shields lowered, and a lightly armed guard placed at the number four airlock.

An hour later, Epsilon approached the Amelia Mary from the stern. When it was two hundred yards from docking, the Epsilon made a maneuver that moved its bow one hundred and eighty from the Earth ship. The Epsilon's speed was lowered to twenty-five feet per second in preparation for docking. When the vessel made contact, there was barely a nudge anywhere on either ship. The crew only knew they were connected when the computer said, "Docking maneuver complete. Airlock pressurized."

The hatches between the ships opened in no more than a few seconds. They slid quietly, and for the first time, two alien but identical species could meet and shake hands.

"Captain Mombassa," the first man through the hatch asked. Once she acknowledged who she was, he continued. "My name is Ambassador Marcus Kingsmen of Terra. It is nice to meet you."

"I am honored to meet you, ambassador," she replied as she gently shook his hand. "May I ask what you are the ambassador of?"

"Captain, I am the representative on Terra of the Unified Territories of Terra," he said with a smile so vast that he didn't know the shock on the captain's face. "Do you have a question?"

"We left Earth six months ago on a mission to see if there was a second legendary planet with the same orbit as Earth. Could this be it," she asked.

Once again, the ambassador smiled. "We have always had the same legend," he said. "We launched a ship fifteen months ago to find out one way or the other. It had a crew of ten, but the ship was not there when we completed our orbit of the star. We assumed it didn't find anything and drifted off into space."

Captain Mombassa looked at the ambassador for just a second. "Mister Ambassador, we have some things we need to discuss," she said. He agreed, and after a quick trip to the infirmary, he was escorted to the bridge.

"Captain, I believe our discussion would better occur on the surface," he suggested. "I will remain on the Amelia Mary to aid you in landing.

The captain thought the same thing, so she got on the intercom and ordered the crews of each respective ship to return to their own vessels, with one exception… Doctor Giovanni was instructed to remain aboard the Epsilon until both crafts safely landed. Now, this was not just a good-faith gesture. The captain also instructed Doctor Giovanni to study the crew and learn as much as she could about them.

As soon as both crews were back aboard their ship, the airlocks were sealed and depressurized, and the two ships separated. The Epsilon was the first to fire its engines, followed closely by the Amelia Mary. "Maintain a distance of five miles," Mombassa ordered.

It would be nearly a day and a half before they entered the planet's atmosphere, so the captain and the crew performed their regular duties. The ship was running at one hundred percent, and the computer said that there were no foreseeable dangers.

The ambassador was escorted to the infirmary for a more complete examination. "Welcome, Mr. Ambassador," a med tech said as Kingsmen entered the room. Could you follow me?" she asked. He agreed to do whatever she required, so she walked him over to one of the tables, asked him to lie down, and then placed connectors to certain places on his body. Then she moved a huge machine over him, pushed a button, and he was immediately sealed in an airtight chamber.

"What are you doing to me?" he demanded to know.

"Mr. Ambassador, this is just a testing chamber," she said. I promise you that you will not be harmed. So, could you please lie still and relax? This all will be done in a few moments." He did as she asked, and five minutes later, the chamber opened. Ambassador Kingsmen was disconnected from the probes and escorted back to the bridge as the tech analyzed the results.

The ambassador sat in a chair next to the captain. "Are all your ships equipped like that," he asked.

"Only the long mission ship has all we have," Mombassa replied. Kingsmen thought momentarily and then asked what she meant by long missions. "We have sent missions to our neighboring planets. Mainly, we just orbited and then returned. This will be our first time landing on another planet except for the moon. We went there way back in the 1970's." Their conversation went on for hours before Captain Mombassa said that it was time to get some sleep. "We have a big day coming up tomorrow," she said just before she took the ambassador to his cabin… the biggest one on the ship other than hers.

The captain could barely sit on the edge of her bed when the intercom sounded. "Captain Mombassa..," it began. This is Ensign Dasvie from the infirmary. I have the results of the tests on Ambassador Kingsmen."

"Ensign what you found," Mombassa asked.

"The scans and tests show that the ambassador is one hundred percent human," Dasvie replied. "Everything is exactly where it should be, and all of the stuff that is supposed to be either high or low is perfect."

Mombassa thanked the ensign, but then she began to think, there's no way that everything in a human body is precisely where it should be. Even a newborn baby has something that just doesn't quite match up with what science says is perfect... so how could he be here? The thought only lasted a minute or two, and then it went into the back of her mind, and a few minutes later, she was sound asleep.

After six hours of sleep, the captain was awakened by a message that only a transmission was coming in for her ears from the Epsilon. It took her a couple of minutes to get the sleep out of her mind and at least appear fully awake. "Patch the transmission to my quarters," she said as she crossed the room to her desk. "Captain Mombassa here," she said as the view screen came to life,

"Hello Urula...Janet here aboard the Epsilon," Doctor Giovanni replied.

"How are things over there," Mombassa asked.

"Well, it's cramped, the food isn't that good, and they have no artificial gravity, but the crew is friendly, and they tried to make me feel at home," Giovanni said. "But that is not why we need to talk."

The captain became concerned. Maybe a contagion aboard would affect the Amelia Mary crew and eventually her earth. Perhaps they had weaponed the scanners couldn't detect. Whatever it could be, she could not think of any way that it would turn out well. "What is it?" she finally asked.

"It's impossible," Giovanni replied. "Well, maybe not impossible, but improbable. Doctor Giovanni was smiling as wide as she could as she continued. "Seriously, you could search until the end of time and not see what I have seen!"

"Janet, what have you found," Mombassa asked again. Her voice was different somehow. Maybe she was caught up in Giovanni's celebration, which would have been strange, especially for the captain. She just wasn't the kind to be drawn into others' emotions.

"It is hard to believe, even for someone like me," Dr Janet Giovanni said with a laugh because she knew how much she was irritating her Captain.

"Janet, if you don't tell me right now, I am going to shoot you out of an airlock when you return to the ship," Urula replied. "I don't want any more joking around... do you understand?"

"Oh, okay," Doctor Giovanni said simply. "Urula, what species is the ambassador?" Mombassa said he was human, and what else could he be?" The doctor told her captain to sit down before he broke the news. Once the captain took her seat, Doctor Giovanni started the news. "I scanned most of the crew and found something interesting. The crew is made up of three different but related species... Homo Erectus, Neanderthal, and Homo Sapiens." Captain Mombassa asked if the scans were correct. "Yes, Urula," Giovanni responded. "I ran each scan three times just to make sure the results came back the same every time I did. There are two extinct species here flying a spaceship from another Earth." The captain said they would continue the conversation on the surface just before she disconnected from the transmission.

The captain sat back on her bed and thought for a minute before she was interrupted by a message that the atmospheric interface was only twenty minutes away. So she got dressed and proceeded to the bridge. "Proceed with landing procedure F-17," she ordered. As the crew began readying for landing, she watched the Epsilon maneuver 180 degrees and fired her main thruster to slow her speed before they hit the edge of the atmosphere. The Amelia Mary used her forward thrusters to perform the same maneuver.

"Five minutes until the atmospheric interface," the navigator said as he closely watched his monitor.

The captain and the rest of the crew strapped themselves in because they knew that re-entry could be a rough ride, even for the most experienced crew.

The bridge crew watched as the Epsilon flipped back into a nose-forward attitude. When the navigator said that there were only thirty seconds left, they watched as the Epsilon raised her nose to an angle of twenty-five degrees. Within seconds of the maneuvers, they watched as the ship in front of them became enveloped in a fire that was so hot that its light made the bridge glow in a bright yellow and orange. The Amelia Mary began to shake violently as it, too, entered the atmosphere.

"Initialize stabilizers," Mombassa ordered as she was thrown to the deck. "Man, all maneuvering thrusters and check the status of all departments." Within seconds, reports came in from all areas of the ship. There were no serious injuries and no damage anywhere on the ship. "Well, that's good news," the captain said as the stabilizers took effect and the flight became smoother. Even though the Epsilon was still burning from friction, she slowly turned toward the left... an act the Amelia Mary followed.

It took both ships another hour to enter the planet's lower atmosphere. The air was clear with several clouds. The ground below was green, with thick vegetation, flowing rivers, and lakes that looked like they were going on forever. Some towns and cities passed by as if they were moving away from the ships. They also gazed down on snow-capped mountains that reminded Urula Mombassa of the many springs and summers she spent with her parents in Europe.

The Epsilon suddenly banked right as they watched and flew into a narrow valley between two mountains. "Captain, we will never fit through there," the pilot said.

"Pull up to an altitude of 10,000 feet and bank right," the captain ordered. "We can't lose sight of the ship!" A second later, the ship's bow rose to an angle of twenty-seven degrees, just enough to clear the mountains but not steep enough that the boat in front of them would fade into the distance. The Amelia Mary made the turn with just inches to spare. Yes, it was frightening since the ship's skin wasn't THAT thick, and the thrusters were more than three inches beyond the skin and could have easily been damaged, but since everything was alright, the captain was paying most of her attention to what she saw after the turn.

"Wow," she said as they turned and leveled off.

Before them was a massive complex with runways stretching more than five miles in any direction. Buildings in the area were so large that they would shadow any building the WSA had in their complexes on Earth. "Oh my God," Louis-Hart said as he rose from his seat at the back of the bridge. "I have never seen anything like that in my life."

"Me neither," the captain said as she watched the Epsilon land and used up most of the runway before coming to a stop and being towed to a 'parking space' in front of the largest building in the complex.

"Welcome to Terra," the ambassador said as he stepped onto the bridge. "The president is waiting for you as soon as you land. You and the rest of your crew will be given an hour to become acclimated, and then you will have lunch and a discussion of your flight."

"Will he explain this?" Mombassa said as she looked down at her swollen belly. "The entire female complements of the crew somehow became pregnant, and we are all due to give birth any time, and I want to know why." Her voice was firm, but she was still polite and respectful, considering this man's position and the fact that they WERE on another planet.

"Believe me… all will be explained," he said with a friendly smile.

"Amelia Mary," a voice said on the radio. "Land your vessel and proceed to area 34 for entry to our visitor's center and processing."

"Where the hell is that?" she asked the ambassador. He smiled and directed her to a space not far from the Epsilon. "Go there," Captain Mombassa ordered the pilot. The pilot followed her orders using just the navigational thrusters, and within ten minutes, the ship landed right where it was directed. "Shut down all nonessential systems," the captain ordered.

Once the officers, crew, and even, despite his objections, the ambassador went through a decontamination process, the hatches were to be opened, and then, for the first time in six months, the crew of the Amelia Mary would be able to breathe unprocessed air, feel the heat of the sun and, at long last, stand on solid ground, which no doubt would make a few of them feel like kissing the ground to make sure it was real and still others to cry and thank their gods for a safe trip. The captain was the first to disembark. Two heavily armed members of the ship's security team and Ambassador Kingsmen followed her. When she stepped on solid ground, the president and an assortment of other officials walked up to meet her.

"Captain Mombassa, it is so nice to meet you," the president said. "My name is Aldrydd Mostyn, President of the Terra Union of Nations."

"It is an honor to meet you, President Mostyn," she replied, shaking the president's hand.

"There is no need for weapons, captain," he said as he looked at her guards. "I promise you that no harm will ever come to you or your crew." Urula Mombassa looked back at her guards. She never said a word…

she just nodded her head, and the men placed their weapons on the ground and stood there watching what was happening. "Please allow the rest of your people to join us." Once again, she looked at her guards, one of which went to the bottom of the steps, and when he nodded his head, the crew came out one by one until the entire crew was finally standing on solid ground. "I am sorry, captain, but you must be processed. Be assured we will talk later," the president said as he stepped away from her.

Several people approached the crew as the president walked away. They separated the men and women into two groups and escorted them through two doors at opposite ends of the smaller building. The crew had questions about what was going to happen since they imagined the worst, but there were no answers. Their escorts did not speak a single word throughout the short walk.

One by one, they walked through the doors. The rooms looked like the standard emergency rooms they all had seen at some point during their lives. That did nothing to allay their fears... in fact, the sight added to their fears by one thousand percent or more.

Captain Mombassa was the first to go through processing for the women. She was taken to a desk, asked for her identification, photographed, and handed an identification card that she could use to order food, drinks... anything she wanted. The last thing the woman behind the desk did was reach over and pull a single hair out of Mombassa's head. From there, she was taken to a private room where she waited for just a couple of minutes before what she assumed was a doctor walked in, followed by Janet Giovanni, who had already been processed. "Urula... relax," she said. "I have already been through it. It is not painful, and you will only be a minute."

The doctor pushed a button, and a machine lowered from the ceiling. "Janet, what is that?" Mombassa yelled. "What is it going to do?" Her thoughts switched from her safety to her babies as the machine wrapped around her abdomen and tightened. She tried fighting as her maternal instincts, as well as her hormones, kicked in full strength. "Let me out of here," she growled. "You are not going to hurt my baby!" She strained against the machine, but it was holding her too tight to allow her to do more than wave her fists and kick her feet.

"No, we would never do that," the doctor tried to reassure her. "It is just a simple test." However, by the time he finished saying that the machine had finished its tests and was headed back into the ceiling. "There now, that wasn't too bad was it?" Captain Mombassa didn't answer, instead he leapt from the table, grabbed the doctor by the collar, bringing up her fist just before Doctor Giovanni grabbed her.

"Urula, all they did was a sonogram, and they took a sample of the baby's DNA to make sure it is okay," she yelled as she kept her friend from killing the doctor. "I swear to you that is all they did… just to make sure the baby is healthy."

Captain Mombassa relaxed a little, as she pulled her fist back and let go of the doctor's collar. "Are you sure," she asked.

"Urula, I swear to you on our friendship that was all they did," Giovanni replied. "

"Your baby is a healthy boy... half human and half homo erectus," stated the unperturbed male Doctor reassuringly, as he quickly left the room.

Janet tried to smile reassuringly, despite instantly observing her friend's look of shock. "Urula just be happy that it is a boy, and he is healthy." The captain was shocked only about the fact they had the technology to read the tests so quickly, yet, for some reason, the fact that her baby was human and Erectus, really didn't seem to bother her that much at all.

"I have a question," Captain Mombassa asked as she got dressed, as a nurse entered the room, and as soon as she was finished dressing, started to escort both Urula and Janet out the door. "Hell no, I have a lot of questions to ask before I go! Then, suddenly, Captain Mombassa started to get angry. "Why the hell won't anyone answer my questions? I have the right to know, what the hell is happening to me and my crew? I want answers!"

"All of your questions will be answered," the nurse said to her soothingly. "It is not that serious."

"NOT THAT SERIOUS," Urula Mombassa yelled as Janet and the nurse tried to calm her down. Then, without warning the captain collapsed to the floor. Doctor Giovanni grabbed the medical bag she always carried with her and immediately went to Urula's aid and checked everything vital such as blood sugar, heart rate, respiration, and reflexes. Everything was normal. Even her eyes were exactly as they should be… still, she was in a deep sleep and she would not wake up.

Doctor Giovanni grabbed the nurse by the collar and slammed her against a row of lockers that lined the wall. "What is wrong with her?" she demanded to know, just as the attending Doctor walked back into the room.

"There is nothing wrong with her," the nurse replied, "It is completely natural." Giovanni repeated the word "natural?" back to her in the form of a question as the nurse, now accompanied by the doctor, sat Doctor Giovanni down on a small bench to explain everything to her. "The baby caused that to happen," the nurse said,

"What?" Giovanni asked.

"I assure you, the baby caused it," the doctor then said. "We have an enzyme in our bodies that does not allow us to become stressed to a level where it maybe be dangerous. Our babies have the enzyme within hours of conception. When Captain Mombassa got so angry, she placed herself and her baby in danger, so the baby used the enzyme to place his mother into a deep sleep."

"How can I wake her up?" Giovanni asked.

"You can't," the doctor replied. "Once the baby feels it is once again safe he will disable the enzyme and Captain Mombassa will wake up in a total state of peace and harmony."

It took more than three hours for the captain to come around. While she waited, Doctor Giovanni managed to get the answers to some of her questions on things she did not fully understand.

"In our world," Janet stated "let me assure you, the different stages of human evolution could not survive together, therefore when the next evolution of man came into existence the previous ones died off. So, how did you evolution take place and become so different to ours?"

The doctor thought for a minute before he answered, it was as if he was trying to figure out a way to explain things to Janet. Finally, he started to tell the Terra story. "In the time before history the three human species were always fighting… usually over food. Just like your world, the numbers of Erectus and Neanderthal declined to such a level where they should have gone extinct. But one concerned Homo Sapiens saw what was happening and went to meet with the leaders of the other species.

The meetings lasted a week, but at the end they emerged with an agreement that there was enough for everyone, and because of this everyone would be better off, if Homo Sapiens, Erectus, and Neanderthal worked together, and everyone shared in anything the then hunters killed. That agreement has changed over the years, but it still means we all work together for the good of everyone. Every community, every individual knows what could happen if we do not take care of each other. No one wants to have the possibility of extinction hanging over their heads, so we all get along."

"That sounds like paradise," Giovanni said. "In our world, every new species of human wiped out the ones who were already there." Immediately the doctor looked in shock as Janet Giovanni continued. "Even after thousands and thousands of years we are still killing each other."

"Over what?" the doctor asked, he could barely get the words out, as he was so shocked, but he really wanted to know.

"It is not so much the people," Janet informed him. "Most of the people in our world don't want war, they want to live in peace, but so many of our leaders do not feel this way. Every section of our world has its leaders, and they all fight over land, money, religion... even food and natural resources. Our leaders have through the ages sent millions of people to fight and die and have even killed additional millions for no good reason, but the annihilation of people they hated. Our leaders in recent years do not even fight in these battles themselves, they sit in their ivory towers deciding our lives, and they are more than willing to let others die for them."

On hearing all this, the doctor became extremely concerned since he knew what was going to happen, so he asked if the violence was mixed in with the DNA of Earth's humans. "No," Giovanni replied. "It is just the greed and ignorance of our leaders. Some have exterminated millions just to gain great power and to do this they feed on their citizens' insecurity, hatred and fear."

"I am so glad that we evolved so differently than that," said the doctor as Captain Mombassa finally stirred and opened her eyes.

"What happened," the captain asked.

"You were stressed and so your baby put you to sleep until you calmed down," Giovanni explained. "It is a protection mechanism which the unborn have developed here to protect themselves as well as the mother. So, I would seriously recommend that you do not get upset, Urula. Or you will be continually sleeping."

As she regained her senses, Captain Mombassa sat up and looked at her friend. "Janet, did I hear you say that my baby is not all humans?" she asked nervously. The minute she asked. Doctor Giovanni nodded her head. "Yes Urula, I did in fact say that!" The moment she stated this, then immediately Captain Mombassa started feeling queasy again and wanted to lie down, but this time Doctor Giovanni was prepared and immediately caught her and did her best to talk her friend into just staying calm and relaxing.

"Just think of it this way," the Terra doctor said. "Your baby is healthy, and as far as I can tell it is a perfect little boy."

"How is this possible?" the captain asked. "Janet, humans cannot breed with other species!"

"Urula… they are not a different species," Giovanni said. "They are more human than any species we have ever found." Then she thought for a moment before she continued. "Believe me, my friend, if only one or two things had gone differently in our human history, we could have been sharing our Earth with the same people they have here on Terra. If only one or two things would have gone differently…" Giovanni didn't know what, but her words calmed the captain down enough so she could be taken to a bus waiting for her outside of the building.

The moment Captain Mombassa boarded the bus, within minutes, all of the men on the crew were escorted from the building and took their seats on the bus. Then, one by one, the women came out. A few were smiling and happy, most came out looking confused or angry, and some even cried. Doctor Giovanni spoke to each female crew member before they stepped onto the bus and did her best to give them all words of encouragement. Unfortunately, in most cases, it did not help.

"I have something to say to you all," Captain Mombassa said as the bus started out. "Walking through her people she continued. "Ladies, we have embarked on a new adventure. For some reason, God has given us each a baby for a reason. I was shocked too when I heard that my baby wasn't fully human, and yes, I was also angry, but I realize that we have been chosen for something, and I know that we are all brave enough to face whatever it is that is going to happen."

That seemed to calm the crew down because instead of crying and being pissed off… now they were once again talking together. Some were bragging about their half-full child and that it was a good thing since their baby had the power of this enzyme to keep the stress level of their pregnancy down. Their only alternative was to sleep and miss the thrill of discovering this new twin Earth Terra.

Having reassured them all, the captain returned to her seat to a round of applause from all the women on her crew. After that died down, they all settled back to watch the scenery and to try and enjoy the ride to their destination, apparently the hotel where they all would be staying.

Once they got to the hotel, the officers and crew were escorted into the lobby. The captain and the other officers were given private rooms while the crew members were paired up and escorted to their rooms. When they opened their doors, they were no doubt surprised because the rooms were not the twelve by fifteen-foot rooms they had known on Earth; these rooms were massive, with a bedroom for each person, a sauna and Jacuzzi, a kitchen and a television that filled one of the walls. On a table in the center of each room, there were drinks and enough food to fill the stomach of each crew member many times over. Outside the windows, they could see clouds drifting around, distant mountains, and even a waterfall that fell into a lake of crystal blue water. "Are these rooms normal for Terra?" one of the crew asked.

"Yes, ma'am," the steward replied. "All accommodations are assigned to give residents the comfort they desire." Then he thought for a minute before continuing. "The homes we live in are designed the same way. Even the poorest of our citizens live in comfort. The president makes sure of that." He didn't give any more time for questions. He politely excused himself and went back to his duties.

Captain Mombassa didn't have time to talk to the help. She walked into her room and headed right for the bed. True, she had been unconscious for a couple of hours, but it had not been relaxing. However, the second her head hit the pillow, she dropped into a deep REM sleep, but even that sleep wasn't relaxing. As her eyes closed, she could feel warmth spread over her body. Her respiration slowed, and her heart seemed to loosen, so her body fell into another world. She was dreaming, though. She dreamt of a land where humans lived as they had thousands of years ago. No electricity, no cars, no timepieces. They just lived. Their skin was pale, their hair was a soft red, and their eyes were snowy white. The captain couldn't hear their words, but she thought they seemed intelligent.

Her dream was so powerful that she walked among the people, talking to them, visiting their markets, and even spending time at a small outside diner watching some people walking by. For most people, a dream like that… that strong… wouldn't be typical, but for Urula Mombassa, it was run of the mill. When she was eleven years old, she went to school in her hometown, and then, once she went to sleep, she was in a town in northern Denmark named Arhus, where she attended school, played with the kids, ate meals with a family, went by the name of Myrra and she learned how to speak fluent Danish. She never told anyone about the dreams or how she learned Danish, but it was clear that she could still travel in her dreams.

About an hour later, there was a knock at the door. The captain woke up to hear Asianne calling her. It was time for her to wake up, as they were being summoned to dinner in the hotel's main dining room.

It took four loads in the elevator to get the officers and crew into the lobby. Once they were all there, they were escorted to the restaurant's entrance. The entrance doors were large, black, and heavy. Two men standing on each side opened them, and the Amelia Mary crew was led in two by two. Each time they entered the room, a man dressed in formal military attire announced their arrival.

Captain Mombassa and Dr. Lois-Hart were the first two through the door. They looked around as they entered. At the head of the room was a long table. The president, whom they had met at the airport, was seated in the center. There were two seats to his right, but the rest of the table was filled with a dozen men and women all dressed in very fancy clothes... the kind you would always see at a state dinner in the White House. They were escorted to their seats, but before they sat down, the president introduced them to the twelve other people at their table. They were the leaders of twelve of the planet's largest territories. Finally, after all the handshaking was finished, they watched as the rest of the Amelia Mary crew were spread out among the other guests.

The topic of conversation at the main table was the differences between Earth and Terra. The captain and the doctor answered questions about Earth and all the various people that populated the planet, as well as the vast differences in culture and religion. The president and the twelve leaders of the main territories wanted to know everything, even going as far as asking about their lives and families.

It was nearly an hour before Captain Mombassa was able to ask the questions that every woman on her crew wanted to know the answer to. "One question I have," she asked the president," Why were we all made pregnant before our trip?" Captain Mombassa wasn't upset or anything like that... she was just curious.

President Mostyn didn't answer the captain directly; instead, he faced the room. "I would like to welcome our guests," he said to all attending guests. Captain Mombassa just asked me a question that deserves an answer.

The women of the Amelia Mary have brought us a gift. They were made pregnant by members of a ship launched from Terra many years ago. Their children have gestated during their voyage and will be born here on Terra." There was a loud murmur in the room, and it was a good guess that it was the women of the Earth. "Although Terrans and Earthers are fundamentally the same, our DNA has some differences. These differences can help Terra by adding new protection and new abilities to our bodies. Those babies will be raised as if they were full-blooded Terrans. They will breed with our citizens and the DNA will spread across the planet in less than one thousand years." The murmuring got louder, but it was drowned out by the sounds of applause from the Terrans at the dinner.

Captain Mombassa was still confused as she sat there listening to whatever the president was saying, but in her mind was that dream she had when she was resting. "Mr. President," she finally started after he had talked for just about fifty-five minutes. "Are we the first aliens to come and meet you?"

"Ah," the president said as he stopped talking and looked at the captain. "There was a ship that landed here about fifty years ago now. They were a species called the Cigelians. We met, and they seemed friendly enough, so we gave them some land about two days' travel from here. We do not interfere with them, and they do not bother us, so everything seems to be working. Why do you ask?"

Urula was sure as hell not going to tell him about her dream, so she simply said that she had heard a couple of kids talking about another group like us and was just curious.

The entire dinner lasted about four hours. It was full of various kinds of food. Drink and entertainment, but the most significant thing was that the Terrans and the crew were talking together, telling stories, and getting to know each other. The more they all talked, the more both sides realized that they weren't that different, but Captain Mombassa still had a strange feeling that she wasn't being told everything. Toward the end of the evening, a young man tapped her shoulder. "Captain Mombassa, would you like to see the rest of our planet away from the city and meet Cigelians," he asked.

"I sure would," she excitedly replied without thinking about what he asked. He smiled, and she smiled. Then, they agreed to meet near the aero port where the Amelia Mary was stored. It was decided that he would have a transport waiting outside the Hotel, and they would meet the following morning. They would travel in a two-person shuttle, and he would show her all that she wanted to see.

Finally, when the formal dinner ended and the president and his distinguished Terran guests had left, the Captain went with her entire crew to a private reception room they had been assigned. She chatted with her crew and officers for a little while; it had been a fantastic day, and at long last, they were starting to relax and come to terms with all that had happened. After half an hour, they all headed to their various assigned rooms. The moment she hit the pillow, she drifted off to sleep. It wasn't a good sleep, though; throughout the night, she felt cramps and contractions, but they were not strong enough to be concerned with, so she just put them behind her and slept the best she could.

In the morning, Captain Mombassa was awakened by the sound of knocking on her neighbor's door to wake them for breakfast. She was one of the last to wake up. Still, instead of going to breakfast, she took the elevator down to the main floor, left the building, got into a transport waiting for her, and went out to the airfield; during the trip, she suddenly began to feel a slight contraction: "Oh my God! " She cried out as she was hit by another contraction that had her kneeling over her seat, but luckily, it soon passed away. At that moment, the birth of her Terran baby was not on her mind; all she knew was her Terran baby was not due yet, and she sure was not going to miss out on seeing all of the highlights of this twin earth and being the first human to meet an alien species.

When she arrived at the aero port in the distance, she observed the small shuttle. Once they entered the aero port, the transport headed straight to where the Amelia Mary was stationed. The transport stopped, and as the driver opened her door, the young pilot she had met the night before stepped forward to greet her. "Welcome, Captain. Are you ready to go?" he asked with a very friendly, warm smile.

They drove in a smaller vehicle to the waiting shuttle. He helped her into the small vehicle and closed the door behind her.

"President Aldrydd Mostyn has informed the Cigelians of your visit.

"I cannot wait to meet them," Urula Mombadds replied as she boarded the two-seat ship, which had already been fueled and warmed up.

"Buckle in, captain," Mombassa'a escort said. "This will not take too long." Within minutes, they were given clearance to leave. The escort, who informed Urula his name was Ethos, pushed a couple of buttons, and the ship lifted into the air and rose to an altitude of nearly twenty thousand feet before turning west and starting across the sky. Gradually, the boat rose to fifty thousand feet, and as it did, its speed increased until the ground below was nothing more than a blur.

"How fast are we going," Mombassa asked as she saw the edge of dawn before them. That shocked her as the sun had risen nearly four hours earlier. Then, even more surprising, within a few seconds, the ship was suddenly enveloped by the darkness of night.

Urula recognized some of the constellations above her, but were hard to follow because of their speed. Her escort never answered her question about their speed, even when the captain saw them heading into the previous night's sunset. Looking at her watch, she saw they had been on a flight for less than twenty minutes. As the ship began to slow, Mombassa wondered how far they had traveled.

"How far have we traveled so far?" she asked. This time, Ethos answered and informed her that the flight had been more than eleven thousand miles. Nothing on Earth could get up to those kinds of speeds, so she then asked about the engines. Once again, there was no real answer. Her escort said that she would be told everything when they returned to the city.

"We're here," Ethos informed her a few seconds later.

Below was an island. It went on as far as she could see, even from altitude. Mombassa guessed it must go on for hundreds or even maybe thousands of miles. At the edges of the island were thick rainforests, and she could see from the air that the interior was more savannah and scrub brush. There were no roads or cities. There were no signs that anyone was inhabiting the land beneath her until she saw smoke coming from just beyond a river a few miles away. Still, the vegetation was so thick that Mombassa couldn't see anything through the canopy.

"How many people live here," Mombassa asked.

"We aren't sure," he replied. "They are autonomous, so they don't have much to do with the rest of us."

Captain Mombassa didn't know why, but somehow, she could understand why these people wanted to be left alone. The statement made her think of Earth and how, even now, they were still finding aboriginal tribes in the rainforests that were untouched and pure. She had always felt an intense sadness whenever they were discovered because without these people even realizing it, it always meant the end of their way of life. So, she was happy that it was not like that here for the Cigelians.

The landing area was just a clearing in the forest. It was barely large enough to hold the ship, but Mombassa's escort was experienced in this site. Hence, the ship settled quickly, and shortly, Mombassa and Ethos disembarked and headed into the jungle. Ethos explained that the landing site was about five miles from the settlement. The walking was rough. Because of the thickness of the foliage, the two of them couldn't see more than maybe five or six feet around them, but even so, Urula felt they were being watched. After a couple of hours, they broke through the jungle and stepped into a village… perhaps the city would be a better term since Mombassa was looking upon thousands of huts covering a distance farther than she could see, and they were primitive.

"What is this," Mombassa asked.

"This is the Cigelian settlement," the escort said with a smile.

"The president told me that they crashed in their spaceship," Urula stated. "Wow, this place certainly does not look like the people here know anything about the wheel and certainly not space travel."

"When we crashed, we decided to live without the technology that brought us here," a voice said from the forest.

Captain Mombassa turned toward the voice and saw a woman stepping into the open. She was slightly over six feet tall, with ivory-white skin, white blonde hair, blue eyes, and soft red lips.

"Hello, Captain Mombassa, my name is Kathalonda. I would like to welcome you to Cigelia. May your stay be peaceful and happy," she said as she lowered herself into a deep bow. Then she rose, took the captain by the hand, and led her into the forest.

At that moment, Urula did not notice that her escort was no longer with her. In fact, she had reboarded the ship and began procedures for take-off.

"This is an important occasion for us, Captain Mombasa, and we do not get many visitors," Kathalonda said. "It is such an honor that you have come to us."

"I am the one who is honored," Mombassa said. "I heard of you while in the city and wished to meet you and get to know your people."

It was still quite a walk to where they were going, and the captain got to see plants and animals that she had not seen in the city...birds with fluorescent feathers, mammals the size of humans, and tiny little lizards that would climb up your legs and lick the salt from your face. Colossal redwood-type trees surrounded the area, some so big that they looked like they were going all the way to

Heaven and back. There were flowers of every color you could imagine and then some. Their scent filled the air with such perfume that Mombassa felt she was in Nirvana as she walked; she could not believe that she could feel that good on his second earth, but even that didn't last long. As she walked, she heard a noise that she didn't expect to hear... the sound of the ship's engines firing up. "What's going on," she asked as the ship she had traveled in lifted off the ground, buzzed overhead, and then headed toward the city.

"You will be fine...I promise you that," Kathalonda said as she cleared away some of the brush to clear the path. "The people of Cigelia are friendly, and we will care for you." That answer didn't answer her question. It made Urula more nervous about the situation than even hearing the engines had done.

"Please follow me," the pretty young girl said as they walked past hut after hut. Most had a fire going inside, probably for cooking, and others were bathing outside in large wooden tubs while children ran up and down the streets playing just like the children did on Earth. Captain Mombassa saw no electric lights, stoves, cars, or anything.

"This is so amazing," Mombassa said. This is how humans lived on Earth more than a thousand years ago." Kathalonda turned and looked at her and asked if there was a problem she could help with. "No," Mombassa said. "I am just amazed at how you and your people live. It is truly unique."

"We have lived like this since long before I was born," Kathalonda said with a smile. "I don't think I would want to live any other way." She showed limitless pride in her community and the way her people lived. She walked the captain and passed home after home. She saw shops with fruits and goods she had not seen back in the city, and everyone smiled at her as they walked by. As if they were welcoming her as one of them.

"Where are we going," Urula asked Kathalonda.

"The center of our land is something you must see," Kathalonda answered. "It is where the elders are seated, and I am sure they will want to meet you." Mombassa was sure of that too, maybe even as much as she wanted to meet them. After all, how many times in her life would she, as the official representative of the Earth, be able to meet a species that came from another planet?

I wonder what's going on back in the city, Mombassa asked herself. *She knew that, once again, she was getting mild cramps that came and went as they walked. They weren't bad at that moment, but they were stronger than they had been before she left the city. What she didn't know, though, was that in the city, each of her crew was* experiencing the same cramps as they were all getting closer to giving birth.

"You do not have long, do you," Kathalonda asked with a smile as she touched the captain's swollen belly. "Motherhood is such a blessing. I have five children of my own. The youngest is nearly a month old now. The oldest is almost seven."

This shocked Mombassa because the woman walking with her looked to be no more than twelve or thirteen.

"Katahalonda, how old are you," Mombassa asked.

"That does not matter," she answered. "Just know that I have been through what you will experience, and if you'd like, I can help you."

Then, the captain suddenly realized that without her escort, Ethos, and the tiny shuttle, she was trapped in this community, away from humans and her crew.

"Kathalonda, how long will my escort Ethos and I visit you? Unfortunately, my contractions seem to be increasing, and I am worried something could be wrong. If I am not back in the city soon."

Kathalonda didn't have an answer. She did not know how to tell Captain Mombassa that her escort, Ethos, had already left and that there was no set schedule for transport from the city.

"Captain, I am sorry to inform you, but your escort, Ethos, has already left us. No doubt he has left for the city and will be returning later."

On hearing Captain Urula Mombassa for the first time, she became afraid. Maybe the president of Terran wanted her away from her people for some reason, she thought. Maybe something bad was going to happen to her crew, and they wanted her out of the way. Oh, how naive she had been. How could she have been so foolish? She was the Captain of the Amelia Mary. How could she have been so stupid as to trust the people of Terran?

At that moment, she could not understand why she had been left in this primitive, isolated place, but she did know that she didn't feel good about what was happening.

A moment or two later, they reached the center of the community. Before her, there were three of the same pale-skinned people with the same white, blonde hair and blue eyes.

"Welcome to our land," the middle one said. "My name is Nabho Khued. I am honored to meet you and welcome you to Cigelia."

Captain Mombassa introduced herself and said she was pleased and honored to visit a land like Cigelia. Even though in the back of her mind, she felt extremely nervous and suspicious of everything happening. Summing up all her courage, she immediately asked. "I am honored to be here, meeting you all, but I am also concerned, so I will ask straight out: am I a prisoner here?"

"Oh, Captain Mombassa, most definitely not," Nabho replied in a shocked voice. Please understand. When someone visits us from the city of humans, they usually stay for a few days to get to know our people, our culture, and our history. It is not very often, though, that we get visitors, so we make their stay something to remember. I hope we can do that for you also."

"I understand, and I hope to get to know you and your people," the captain replied, even though her concern for her crew made her determined that she would not stay very long.

Her cramps were getting worse, but they still weren't disabling, so she simply gritted her teeth and kept smiling. Even Nabho and Kathalonda could see the captain was in some pain, so after some handshaking, she was taken by Kathalona's visitor's hut and persuaded to lie down on a very comfortable bed and take a short nap.

"Captain Mombassa," a sweet voice said a few hours later. "Are you alright?"

"I'm fine," the captain replied as her eyes cleared. She saw Kathalonda's face smiling down at her. I guess I was just a little tired." She knew that wasn't true; in fact, she was at the very beginning of labor, and she knew it.

"If you can, I would like to show you something," Kathalonda said as she took Mombassa'a's hand and helped her from the bed. The captain said that she would love to go for a walk. She knew from her sister that walking was a good way to get labor going. "I think you are going to enjoy this, " said the smiling Kathalonda.

They walked a small distance to what looked like a school. There were children in the yard. They were playing, yelling, and having fun, just like the children on Earth. Mombassa swore later that she saw some of the kids playing monkeys in the middle, which was a very similar game to soccer. A couple of the older kids, the captain figured they would be equal to seniors in high school back home, were off to the side, and they were talking, holding hands, and kissing the way kids do. "This reminds me of home," Mombassa said.

Kathalonda smiled and nodded her head to some of the kids playing nearby. They came rushing over like they heard someone was handing out chocolate. They gathered around the captain. They were all talking and telling her about their lives while asking questions about her. A couple had small groups of tiny purple flowers they presented to her as gifts. Others gave her little hand-made things like beads and other trinkets. She thanked every one of them. Each time she did, they jumped up and hugged her. Then they all gathered close and sang her a song. It was in the language of the Cigelians. She couldn't understand a word, but it was beautiful, and she loved it anyway.

Afterward, she was taken to a large building with a fireplace opposite the room. She saw several women cooking meat and vegetables she had never seen before. The captain learned later that she was being served a dish reserved for the most special occasions.

"What is that?" Urula asked.

"We call it Marlei," Kathalonda said. "It is vibrant and spicy, but it tastes very nice. I know that you will like it, and so will your baby." That didn't answer the captain's question, so she asked exactly what the dish was made of.

"It is made from fish we gather from the ocean. We grow seasoned with herbs and spices in the community gardens, and several farms provide them to us. They are all grown without chemicals, and every plant is given the respect its soul deserves, as before we process it, we ask it if we may use it for our nourishment."

"Oh my God," Mombassa screamed as she bent over at the waist and fell to the ground. Her contractions had undoubtedly increased, coming about every twenty minutes. "I do not understand why, but I think my baby's coming! I am so sorry, I need to get back to the city. My crew must be giving birth, too! Please get in touch with my escort Ethos to return and get me immediately so I can be with my female crew now?"

"Captain Mombassa, I am so sorry, but we do not have a way to contact the city or even a way to get you back to the city," Kathalonda said as she took the captain's hand.

"Can't you call them," Mombassa asked with a touch of panic in her voice. "Can you get them to come and get me and take me back?"

Kathalonda then said they had no way to contact the city and never had any desire. The town rarely contacted them when they needed to, so she was very sorry.

Captain Urula Mombassa suddenly realized that, due to her own stupidity and ego, she was now stuck with a species she had never dealt with. Suddenly, her pain increased, and she yelled out loud, "I think I am having my baby. " She yelled, "Please help me."

The Cigelians gathered around her. Two of them took her by the arms and walked her around the plaza and into one of the cleanest buildings.

"Captain," Kathalonda started. "Believe me, you are lucky to have your baby here rather than in the city. Your baby will be healthier and safer being born here, and we are truly pleased to be able to assist you with your birth."

Kathalonda's words helped the captain relax, but she was still apprehensive about the whole thing. Why was she picked out to be brought to the middle of nowhere and dropped… abandoned.. would be a better word. What was happening with her crew? Indeed, if she was in labor, so would all the pregnant women on her crew. That thought scared her more that she was afraid of giving birth… what was happening, and why wasn't she allowed to know?"

Back in the city, each of the women was going into labor one by one. Some had a rough time, mostly the virgins who were not atomically ready to give birth since they had never had the sex necessary to make the proper changes. In contrast, others had labors that lasted only a couple of hours once they started. A few had twins, and one woman even had a set of triplets. All the babies were healthy when they were born, which would be uncommon if not impossible on Earth; all realized there must have been something in the Terran DNA that prevented any possible prenatal problems.

"I have never seen anything like this," Dr. Giovanni said as she rushed from one delivery room to another. Then she looked at one of the nurses and laughed. "I didn't sign up for this. A broken toe, the flu, or something like that, but never so many pregnancies. I must write a paper on this when I get back."

By the time she was done, there had been seventeen births. Six were Homo Sapiens, three were Homo Erectus, and the rest were Neanderthal, but even though all of the babies were different species, they were all beautiful. Within minutes, they were cuddled up with their mothers, feeding for the first time, and a couple opened their eyes and smiled.

While Janet Giovanni was helping with the deliveries, new mothers, and babies, one of the councils approached her and asked her to please meet with him after all of the babies were born. She agreed to meet with him, but she did tell him that it would be hours before she would be able to get away. "I understand," he said. Just make sure we talk. It is critical to you, your crew, and their babies."

"I'll be there," Doctor Giovanni promised. "Just to let you know, I have some questions for you, and I think they are pretty important, too."

The counselor nodded politely and said he would answer her questions to the best of his ability. And do not worry about Captain Mombassa; she was primarily cared for by experts. Relieved about her friends' welfare, Doctor Giovannie thanked him and returned to work caring for all the women she was responsible for.

Unfortunately, for some of the women, though, the glow of motherhood was already starting to wear off, even though it had been just a couple of hours since they had given birth. It was mainly the women who had given birth to non-homo sapiens who were having second feelings about their children.

Doctor Giovanni went from room to room, talking to each of the women, trying her best to get them to bond with their babies, but for some, it would be hard, if not impossible.

A few hours later, Doctor Giocanni finally met with the council. They started one by one to try to converse with her, but she would have no part in it. She wondered why Urula had not been seen or contacted after her baby's birth and why she had not been invited to the meeting. "Where is Captain Mombassa," she demanded to know. "I do not want to hear anything else until I know where the captain is!" Now, Giovanni was usually a calm person, but her temper was being strained, and she wasn't as much asking as demanding to know what she wanted to know, and she wasn't going to be stonewalled.

"She went out of the city to see what Terra has to offer," one of the councilors answered. "She has an escort; if anything were wrong, she would be brought back immediately."

"Look," Giovanni said. "If she is as far along in her pregnancy as the rest of Amelia Mary's crew were, she must have already delivered; I am now very concerned as you had assured me previously that she was having the best care possible. How can that be? Now it seems she is isolated far away, and not as I had thought in safe here in this city being looked after by your well-trained Doctors."

"Believe me," replied the counselor. She could not be safer! She is with the Cigelians, who are spiritualists, and we have been assured she is very happy with the care she has been given. A newborn child means everything to the Cigelians."

"Oh yes, Doctor Giovanni, rest assured she is very safe, and her baby will also receive the best care possible, " another councilor said.

Despite all their reassurances, Janet Giovanni knew something was wrong, something she was not being told. She also knew that her dear friend Captain Mombassa might be in real trouble, but as a guest in Terra, there was nothing she could really do if she wanted to protect the rest of the female crew there. So, she just turned and left the chamber without saying another word or giving the council a chance to say anything.

Where is she? Janet wondered as she headed to the area where all her new Mothers were nursing their babies. *She would never just leave her crew... not at a time like this.* Fortunately or unfortunately, after that, Doctor Giovanni did not have time to worry any further, for there was a batch of females needing her help, and they came first.

Back in Cigeliara, Captain Mombassa's pains were getting much worse. She was going to have her baby, and she knew she wouldn't have time to get back to the city, even if the ship arrived to pick her up at that moment. It was just too late. "Kathalonda," she screamed even though the girl wasn't any more than maybe ten feet away. "I need you. I can't do this by myself!"

"I am here, Captain," Kathalonda said. "I will help you all that I can, but I am too young and inexperienced to deliver your baby for you. We have a woman who can help you if you want me to get them?" Mombassa asked if Kathalonda could send someone else because she did not want to be alone, even for a moment.

"Kathalonda," Urula whispered. "Please call me Urula. We will be great friends, at least for a while." She barely got the words out before another contraction hit, and it was many times harder than the ones she had experienced before. Tears were in her eyes, and her fingernails dug into Kathalonda's arm and hand.

It took less than five minutes for the midwife to arrive. It was fast, but the captain's contractions were coming no more than two minutes apart by the time she got there. "I guess you're having a baby, aren't you," the midwife asked as a joke that fell on unappreciative ears.

"Are you an idiot," Mombassa yelled as her grip tightened on Kathalonda's arm.

"Relax, Urula…it is okay if I call you that," the midwife asked with a smile. Once Mombassa said yes, it was alright, and the midwife continued. "Females of every species have been doing the same thing for millions of years, and I need you to relax… it will make everything much easier."

That was not going to work… not at all. The captain was scared, and words would not help, so the midwife looked at Kathalonda and silently nodded.

"Are you sure you need me to do this?" the young girl asked.

"Kathalonda," the midwife started. "You have to. She has to calm down, and she has to calm down now before she harms herself or the baby. You don't want that to happen... do you?" Of course, Kathalonda didn't want this, so she reluctantly agreed to do what the midwife thought had to be done.

"Urula," Kathalonda said. "My family has been Cigelians for more than a thousand generations, and we have learned many things to help in times such as this. Do you trust me?" The captain nodded as the young girl touched Urula's chest.

"Please listen to my voice," Kathalonda whispered as she began massaging the captain's chest, letting her fingers touch her skin, kneading her muscles, and stroking gently. "You know there is a place where you go to find where you were happy, and all of your thoughts are pleasant. Close your eyes, slow your breathing, and go to that place. It is so warm and so beautiful. You are there all alone, listening to the music of the spirits, smell the scents of nature, and feel the sun's warmth. It is paradise, and you are there." The midwife watched Captain Mombassa's breathing slow, her muscles relaxed, and a slight smile crossed her face.

"That is good," the midwife said. "You have to keep her relaxed." Even though the captain was utterly relaxed, her contractions were still as muscular and as close together as ever, but she couldn't feel the pain. In her mind, the experience was pure pleasure. Even when the baby started coming and the head was crowning, Captain Urula Mombassa was still as happy as possible. From the time when Kathalonda began her "treatment," it was only about ten minutes before a scream filled the room and a new baby was brought into the world. "That's it," the midwife said as she took the bay over and cleaned it up.

"Is it over?" Urula asked as Kathalonda stopped massaging her.

"You have a beautiful baby boy, Urula," the midwife said as she handed the baby over to the captain, who immediately lowered her shirt and began feeding her new son. "So, what are you going to name him," she asked.

"Chikelu," she answered. It was the name of my father and his father before him." Kathalonda asked what Chikelu meant. The proud captain of the Amelia Mary and her newly born was more than happy to explain that since the child was such a blessing, the name she chose was not only a family name but also meant "created by God." To Captain Mombassa, that was exactly what her son was… a creation of God.

Urula and little Chikelu were allowed to sleep the rest of the night, and since his Mum had a lot to do in the morning, they both needed every moment of rest they could. Chikelu was very understanding and only cried once in the night. Soon, he was fed and sung back to sleep by his very proud and pleased mother. Who would have thought a journey to a distant planet in the Amelia Mary would provide her with a son? By the time the captain had given birth, the female members of her crew were in their hospital room. Most were taking the time to bond with their babies, but some wanted nothing to do with their children, and a few even threatened to destroy this creature if they were not immediately removed from their sight.

Naturally, Doctor Giovionni disapproved of anything going on, but even though she was second in command, no one was listening to her, and each woman was in her little world, no matter how good or bad that world was. "What is going to happen to the babies the mothers don't want?" she asked as she walked from room to room, checking on her patients.

"We have thought of that problem with this experiment," a nurse said. "we knew some of your mothers might have second thoughts as they were secretly impregnated, and we even knew some might even be afraid of they had given birth to, and wish to destroy their children so we have arranged for these babies given to various Terran families who are unable to have children of their own. So be assured, that is what we have arranged in case of this emergency of rejection by their mothers… they will be given a happy life with those who will love them.".

By now, the rest of the council had arrived at the hospital to check on the babies and their condition.

"Those babies…the ones you are taking and the wanted babies are citizens of my Earth as much as they are Terrans," Giovanni said.

"We do know that, doctor," one of the female council members said. "We have had children of your planet living here for centuries, and they have always been loved and raised as we would children born of our people… just as we will the children born of your crew."

Janet wondered if they had stolen children from Earth centuries ago. Oh dear, where is Urula? Giovanni thought. She is the one who should be handling this, and they won't help me find her. Something is going on, and I need to find out what.

"Well, as officer in charge until Captain Mombassa returns, I assure you that I will not allow those kids to be touched until Captain is back here," she stated firmly. It seemed that she had missed something... something that the council member said was not like her. Instead of arguing, Giovanni left the room and then the hospital and went back to her room to rest and think.

Captain Mombassa finally had her strength back, and she enjoyed being taken care of by some of the Cigelian women. They were primping her, bathing her, and covering her body with scented oils. While she was relaxing, Chikelu was also being pampered. He was bathed and powered, fed a rich concentration of natural vitamins that all

Cigelian babies were fed on their first day of life.

"When can I leave here?" Mombassa asked. She was extraordinarily relaxed, considering everything that was going on in her mind. She had so many concerns for her crew and their new kids. She had thoughts of Chikelu and how she would raise him, how to get back to the city, off this planet, and back to Earth, and what she would find when they got back there.

Once again, she was told the same thing…there was no communication with the city, and the ship that brought her to the village may show up in minutes, but it may be hours, days, or even months.

"Honestly, Urula, there is no way to know when someone wants to escape the city," Kathalonda said. Then she asked the captain to let her know when she was available because she wanted to show her something she may be interested in, but she wouldn't tell the captain what it was. All she would say is that the baby would have to be taken care of by the women who were taking care of him already, as the trip would be too rough on a newborn baby.

True, Mombassa had just given birth, but she was a strong woman, and she had been resting for many, many hours, so a short trip might do her some good, clearing out the cobwebs. So, despite the midwife's advice, Mombassa and Kathmonda went out for the day.

It was a nice, restful walk through some of the most beautiful forests on the planet, but even so, Captain Mombassa wasn't able to enjoy what she was seeing because she was worried about her crew and what was happening to them back in the city. She reconciled to the fact that there was nothing she could do at present. Urula appreciated them exploring and seeing firsthand what Terra was all about.

"Where are we going," she asked. Kathalonda didn't answer directly. Instead, she said that it was something the captain had to see.

It was about an hour outside the village when they came upon a group of about a hundred huts. They were much like the ones back in the town, but the inhabitants differed. They were all humans... different races and species, but still they were all humans. "What is this," the captain asked.

"They are all from the city. They were brought here to visit us and were never taken back," Kathalonda said.

Those words hit Mombassa like a brick wall. "Never taken back," Mombassa asked. "What do you mean by that?"

"The ship that brought you here," Kathalonda started. "It comes, drops someone off, and then leaves before anyone can get on to leave."

"Like me," Mombassa asked.

"Exactly like you," Kathalonda responded. "We consider them Cigelians. They are our people, just as you and Chikelu are now."

XXXXXXXXXXXXXXXXXXXXXXXXX XXXXXXXXX

Captain Mombassa liked that. It was just the right thing to hear at that moment. Although the people living there were prisoners...not of the Cigelians but rather of the people back in the city—and she was now one of them, in her heart, she knew that the situation wasn't going to last THAT long. "How long have they been here?" Mombassa asked.

"Some just a cycle or two," Kathalonda said. "Some were here long before I was born." She pointed to one gentleman sitting by a fire in the center of the village. "He has been here the longest...more than forty cycles. If I remember right, he was once the council leader, but when he lost power, the people who took over sent him here as a punishment."

The captain walked over to him. "Sir, may I speak with you a moment," she asked. Once he nodded his head, she sat down. That was hard for her to do since his clothes were dirty, old, and smelled terrible. He was filthy, his hair was long and unkempt, his eyes glazed over, and he had a dead stare. "Are you okay," she asked as she took his hand. Once again, he nodded his head. Then it became apparent that the man she was sitting next to either didn't want to or couldn't talk.

"He has given up," Kathalonda said. "He used to be full of spirit, but that was long ago." Urula smiled slightly as she listened and looked into the man's eyes. "His name is Jarad," she said.

Mombassa stroked his cheek. "Jarad, I am going to get us back to the city…I promise you that," she said. Then she got angry. "Kathalonda," she yelled. "I want to know the next time the ship returns to the village. I am going to get these people home." Then she took the time to ask each one if they would go back to the city if she could find a way. There were only a couple who said that yes, they did want to go back. The rest were happy living without technology. Urula knew the feeling but also knew she had to return to her crew and home.

Doctor Giovanni was searching the city for the captain. She started going from house to house, asking if anyone had seen Mombassa walking around. Every answer was the same. The people had heard of her and the Amelia Mary, but no one had seen her. Then she had an idea. Rushing back to the hotel, Giovanni grabbed a hairbrush from the captain's bag.

"What are you doing?" a crewmember asked as the doctor started to look for the door.

"I am going to find our captain," Giovanni answered. "Get Louis-Hart and Asianne and have them meet me in the infirmary aboard the ship." The crewmember confirmed the order and started to ask a question before he left, but he was quickly interrupted and told not to ask or say anything, to go and find the officers, and do what he was told.

The crewmember did his job because, within half an hour, both Louis-Hart and Asianne were walking into the infirmary.

"Janet, what's up," Asianne asked.

"Captain Mombassa is missing, and we are going to find her," Giovanni said as one of the computers came to life. She took the brush from her pocket. She carefully looked and looked again and again until she found just what she was looking for…one of Urula's hair with a viable root ball on the end.

Neither of the other two had any other questions, so the doctor took the hair and placed it into one of the many machines.

It would take about thirty minutes for the computer to run the necessary tests, so

Giovanni, Louis-Hart, and Asianne went down to the galley and made themselves something to eat. While they ate, they could hear noises from outside the ship. "What is that?" Arianne asked.

"I heard they were going to work on the damage on the ship," Louis-Hart said. "It has to be the workers."

After thirty minutes passed, Giovanni went up to get the results. "Computer, results," she ordered.

"The sample belongs to Captain Urula Mombassa," the computer responded. "Captain Mombassa is currently assigned to command the W.S.S. Amelia Mary. Mission classified."

"That's all I needed to know," Giovanni said as she smiled at her friends. Then she looked at the science officer. "Have the computer scan to find her DNA signature." The officer did as he was told, and it didn't take long for the computer to respond.

"Captain Urula Mombassa is located at 13.45.00 degrees north and 87.10.35 degrees west," the computer responded.

"How far is that away," Arianna asked.

"18311.116 kilometers," the computer told the shocked trio. Giovanni ordered the computer to confirm the findings. "Captain Urula Mombassa is moving to her location, so my findings are correct: within one hundred meters."

"Computer, is the Captain's Yacht available and prepared for flight?" the doctor said. Once she confirmed that the small ship was available and prepared, an important thought came to her that she just had to ask. "Does anyone know how to fly the ship?" she asked. None of them knew how, but Asianne came up with the answer.

"We need to get a pilot or engineer," she said. Unfortunately, all of them were back in the city, and it was way too dangerous for any of them to go back and retrieve one of them. The discussion lasted a good hour before Asianne said something else. "There is an engineer aboard," she said. The others mumbled before, one by one, they remembered the one crew member still on board…Lieutenant Kevin Kiselow!

"Computer," Giovanni said. "Status of Lieutenant Kevin Kiselow."

"Lieutenant Kevin Kiselow is in stasis tube seven," the computer replied.

"What is the shortest time necessary to revive Lieutenant Kiselow safely," she asked.

"Shortest time to safely revive Lieutenant Kevin Kiselow…eleven minutes, thirty-seven point five seven two seconds," the computer said. "Recommended time for revival one hour."

"Revive Lieutenant Kiselow as fast as safely possible," Giovanni ordered. The computer verified the order and began the procedure to revive the lieutenant. Then she turned to Asianne and Louis-Hart and told them to ensure that the captain's yacht would be ready for an immediate and speedy launch as soon as Kiselow was strong enough to fly the ship. Then, the conversation began about how they would tell Kiselow what was happening. Giovanni said that since she was the interim ship commander, she would tell him everything he needed to know. Then, as the computer did its job, Giovanni and the others began preparing for the flight.

Finally, Kiselow's stasis tube opened, and he stepped out into a chamber that, except for him, was empty. He looked and found an intercom. "Who's here," he said as he pushed the blue button in as hard as possible.

The voice that replied had a total sense of urgency. "Kiselow, I am glad you are awake," Asianne said back to him. We are on the captain's yacht. You have to get up here immediately, if not sooner."

The computers and command consoles aboard the small ship began coming on as Kiselow stepped through the hatch and locked it behind him. He just stared as Giovanni ordered to set a course to land within five hundred meters of Captain Mombassa. "Yes, Captain," the computer replied. "Landing site detected and course plotted—five hundred thirty-two meters west of Captain Mombassa'a's current location.

"Kevin, can you fly this thing," Giovanni asked. Kiselow said that he was one of the people who helped design and build the craft, so he would have no problem flying it...especially if Captain Mombassa were in trouble.

As the hatches opened at the back of the ship, guards came running from the buildings. They were armed, and their weapons pointed at the small ship. "Shields up," Kiselow said as the ship lifted.

"GET US OUT OF HERE," Giovanni yelled.

They felt the force of the engines roar as they went up to one hundred percent thrust. This ship was built as a shuttle...not for extended flight in an atmosphere as thick as Terra's. That meant that the hull would heat up quickly due to the friction.

"How long can we travel at this speed?" Louis-Hart asked. Kiselow did some figuring on his pad as well as in his head and came up with an approximate time of one point three hours. And what is the time to our landing site?" Again, Kiselow did some math that no one else would ever be able to understand and came up with an approximate arrival time of one hour and fifty-two minutes.

Kiselow looked at the doctor, who had been listening to what the two were talking about. "Decrease speed by ten percent," she said. She realized that the decrease would still allow them to make the flight in a little over two hours and still protect the ship's structure.

"Giovanni hadn't turned the radio for the first fifteen minutes of the flight, but he finally decided that if the captain had a radio and wanted to get ahold of anyone, they would be able to hear him and respond. As soon as the switch was flipped, a strange voice came over. "Unidentified craft," it started. You're being tracked and are being ordered to return to the airport, or you'll be shot down."

"We are officers of the W.S.S. Amelia Mary," Giovanni said. "We are on a mission to recover our commander. If you send ships after us or fire upon us, we will consider it an act of war, and we will defend ourselves." Now, she knew that the captain's yacht didn't carry weapons and its shields were enough to defend itself against an attack, but she was bluffing, and everyone on the bridge knew it.

A few Terran fighters buzzed the ship, but their aggression was minimal. That was lucky for the small boat because there was no way they could outfly or outmaneuver a fighter, and no one on the crew was experienced enough to get into a dogfight anyway. However, after they heard Giovanni's transmission, they backed off to a safe distance and finally returned to their base.

"What are we going to do when we find the captain," Asianne asked.

"Whatever we have to do," Giovanni answered, and she meant that. No matter what they were facing…no matter how dangerous…they would get their captain back, and they all knew it.

The ship flew on and on, making minor corrections to its course as it proceeded. "Destination in two hours," the computer announced. "Scans show many living beings, mostly unidentified, several human life signs away from the main group."

"What in the hell is she into down there," Asianne asked. No one knew the answer to that, and no one wanted to hazard a guess, but they all knew that they had to be armed to the teeth when they landed. One by one, they went to the armory. Each took a pair of small hand weapons and heavier weapons just in case.

When the ship was five minutes from the Cigelian community, the engines lowered the power until barely noticeable on the monitors. It also dropped in altitude until it was just barely above the treetops, making the ship invisible to any tracking systems they might have.

Suddenly, the radio kicked on. "Earth ship...you are forbidden to land anywhere except in your designated landing site," the voice said. "Return to the city immediately and obey the commands of your escort fighters."

Giovanni was pissed. They were close to the captain and would NOT return or obey any "orders" until the captain was aboard. She hit the button on the communications console. It was an angry smile, and she flashed at her crew. They knew what it meant, and they all agreed without saying a word. Giovanni bent over the console and said just three words. She said, "Go to hell," then broke off communications.

Down below, the Cigelians had seen the ship and heard the engines long before it was near the landing site. They had all gathered to welcome the ship and its passengers...that is, except for one Cigelian. Kathalonda took off, running down the path to inform Captain Mombassa that another shuttle was headed for the village.

"Do NOT fire unless you are attacked," Giovanni ordered. "Our first goal is to get the captain and get her and her baby out of here." The others agreed, but their weapons were all set in the highest settings, just in case. "Kevin, stay behind and keep the engines ready for an immediate launch." He also agreed.

Finally, the ship set foot on the landing site. The Cigelians gathered around, getting closer and closer to the ship until the hatch began to open. Then, they all backed off to a safe distance except for one who walked closer to the ship.

Giovanni stepped through the hatch. Her eyes moved across the hundreds of people standing beneath her. Louis-Hart and Asianne followed her closely…their guns were armed and leveled at the one Cigelian standing before them. "Where is Captain Mombassa," Giovanni yelled. Out of the corner of her eye, she saw Louis-Hart's finger twitching on his trigger. She looked at him and sternly ordered him to move his finger away until trouble began.

"Your captain and her baby are safe," the man replied. "We do not harm visitors."

"Visitor," Giovanni asked in a sarcastic tone. "She was taken from the city and has not been allowed to return. We do not call that visiting…we call that kidnapping."

"If we could have, we would have taken her back to you," he said. We were not holding her here. I give you my word of honor on that." He started walking toward the ship, and as he did, Louis-Hart and Asianne aimed their weapons directly at the center of his head.

"Get ready," Giovanni said as the man kept walking.

He was ten feet away from Giovanni when a familiar voice broke the silence. "What in the hell is wrong with you," the voice said. "These are good people, and you will not cause them any harm." They both lowered their weapons as Captain Mombassa stepped through the crowd. Giovanni, Louis-Hart, and Asianne stared momentarily as Mombassa yelled at them to drop their weapons. "I will not allow these people to be harmed…do you understand that?"

"Urula, welcome," the man said as he took her hand. She stood next to him as Kathalonda walked up to her, holding Chikelu.

"Come down here and meet the Cigelians," the captain said politely. "They have helped Chikelu and me ever since I arrived here." Weapons dropped to the ground, and the officers of the Amelia Mary walked down the stairs and shook hands with the first non-human aliens they had ever met. However, the captain looked over at Giovanni with a look of disappointment. "Janet, I expected more of you than to come with weapons drawn," she said.

Captain Mombassa and the other went with a couple of the Cigelian leaders and Kathalonda into one of the buildings where they could talk. She explained how she had been treated and about the others who had been dropped off and forgotten.

"The government said that they had no idea what happened to you," Giovanni said.

"Mostyn was no help at all except he told us one thing...he said that the babies born to our crew were citizens of the Terran people and belonged to them." The captain asked if everyone had given birth. "Yes," she replied with a smile. "They were all born within an hour of each other. I attended each of the births, and all babies were healthy as far as I could tell, but I couldn't be sure about the three species of humans involved."

Mombassa asked a few more questions, but all the answers she got made her madder and madder until she reached her limits.

"The thing is, Urula," Giovanni started. "A few of the mothers didn't want their children and gave them up as soon as they were born."

"That makes no difference," Mombassa said. "Those children are Earthlings who will return to Earth with us. There will be no discussion about that. They are going with us." Then, she began discussing the situation in the village. "We will take anyone who wants to return to the city with us."

"Captain," Kiselow said as he finally joined the rest of them. "We have the captain's yacht. There was barely enough room for us. We cannot take anyone back with us...not right now." The captain thought for a minute, going through the ship's layout, and she agreed with the engineer. There was not going to be enough room.

"Kathalonda, go tell those people I will be back for them as soon as possible," she said. I will be back, I promise." Kathalonda didn't wait; she ran down the human community to deliver the message.

After they ate, drank...and danced a little, they settled into the captain's hut for the night. Not that there would be much sleep between Chikelu's crying and discussions about how to handle the many situations that had come up. Finally, just as the sun rose, they fell asleep, but even that was not meant to be.

About an hour later, a young boy burst into the hut. "Captain...captain," he was yelling. "There is another ship coming, but it is not the one that usually comes. This one is different. It is out over the river but will be here soon."

The captain didn't wait to hear more; she woke the others up. They had to get their ship out of there, and they had to get it out immediately. *I don't know who they are or what they want, but she thought I would not be in the ground to find out.*

Kiselow didn't wait long enough even to get dressed. He ran across the village in his underwear while struggling to carry his clothes. Asianne and Louis-Hart were on his heels, with Mombassa taking up the rear. "How far are they away," she yelled.

"About thirty minutes," a voice replied, but it was doubtful that she heard the answer. She was running too fast and too focused for that.

"As soon as I get in, shut that door and lift off," she ordered. The engines roared, and she felt the ship shaking as she stepped through the hatch. Let's go!" She was nervous and shaking herself as she sat on the bridge. The scanner in front of her showed the ship no more than ten minutes away. "I was a ninety-degree course," she ordered.

"Captain…," Kiselow said.

"Yes," the captain replied. "Get us straight up and out of the atmosphere as soon as we launch.

He pushed a single button as the ship lifted into the air. The bow lifted, and the boat lunged ahead. The force on their bodies felt as if they were being torn in half, but they were still able to breathe, and that was enough to keep them alive.

The ship climbed to well over sixty thousand feet in less than ten seconds before it leveled off. "Show me what's happening," the captain ordered. The view screen flashed on, and they saw several ships approaching the Cigelian community. They all stopped at different positions around the village. One by one, a shuttle launched from each ship, landing inside the forest that surrounded the town. They could not do anything about whatever was happening down on the surface, so Mombassa ordered Kiselow to return to the city as fast as the ship could take them.

"Now, tell me what has been happening," the captain asked. She was feeding her baby, but her attention was strictly focused on what her officers told her.

"Urula…," Louis-Hart started. "…the ships have left the village and are returning to the city. They are approximately fifteen minutes behind us."

"Can they track us," Mombassa asked.

"No sir," Kiselow answered. "Their scanners are not as advanced as ours, but their speed is currently ten percent above ours." Mombassa thought for a moment and typed in something into her computer.

"Alien ships will contact us in twenty-three minutes and seven seconds," the computer said. "Recommend evasive action."

"What evasive action," she asked. Kiselow didn't wait for the computer to answer. He said he thought that making a ninety-degree turn, circling the city, and coming in the opposite direction. Mombassa and Asianne looked at Louis-Hart and Dr. Giovanni, and silently nodded at each other. "Kiselow," Mombassa said. "Make that turn immediately."

The ship didn't make the long sweeping turns it usually made. Instead, it turned in less than fifty feet, slamming the officers onto the bulkhead. Luckily, no one was hurt other than some minor bumps and bruises.

"Captain, the ship went past us, Kiselow said, but that was a little premature because the ship, now in front of them, turned and stopped no more than five miles before them. "Captain...," Kiselow said nervously.

"I see them," Mombassa said as her eyes locked onto her console's view screen. Then, she ordered her ship to come to a complete stop.

Both ships were face-to-face. Neither knew what the other had planned, so the captain decided to wait. "Computer, scan the meapons on that ship," Mombassa ordered.

"All weapons on the ship are offline," the computer replied. There is no sign of hostility within the ship." Then there was a pause. "The other ship is scanning us. Would you like me to block the scan?"

"No, take no action," Mombassa ordered. The rest of the officers looked at her. There was confusion over what she was doing and why she was doing it. The captain noticed the looks and decided it was best to explain even though she was not used to explaining her actions to anyone. "I do not want to do anything to show any aggression," she said. "This is their world, and they have the weapons behind them, and they have our people, and I will not put them at risk." The officers all agreed and waited to see what would happen next.

The other ship moved closer until it was no more than three hundred yards from Amelia Mary's shuttle. "Captain Mombassa," a voice came over the radio. Please lower your shields. I wish to come over and speak to you." The voice sounded familiar, but Mombassa asked who she was talking to anyway. "This is Marcus Kingsmen," he replied. We need to talk."

"Come over," Mombassa said. Just you and no weapons." Although her voice was friendly, it had a severe tone that conveyed her message.

Less than five minutes later, the hatch on the Captain's Yacht turned, and the ambassador stepped onto the bridge. He was searched before his second foot hit the deck, and after that, he was allowed to approach the captain.

Mombassa approached the ambassador, followed closely by Giovanni, Asianne, and Louis-Hart. Kiselow remained at the pilot's station, but his ears weren't paying attention to the console. They were tuned into what was happening behind him.

"Well, ambassador, what do you want to talk about," Mombassa asked.

"I have a feeling I know what you are planning," Kingsmen said. Mombassa asked him what he thought he knew, and he quickly said that he figured that she felt sympathy for the humans in that village and wanted them to return to the city. She couldn't deny that, and then he explained why they were there. "I arranged for them to be taken there just as I had arranged the same for you," he said. Our leaders are paranoid and have been since the Ciglians arrived. Anyone who talks about diplomatic relations or asks questions about them is sent there as a punishment. Some of them have been there so long that they no longer exist in our world."

"She got sent there for asking too many questions," Asianne asked.

The ambassador, yes, that was the reason, but more than that, Mostyn was talking about locking her away in a prison to die. "I sent her to save her life. I am sure that the president would have ordered her killed because if an off-worlder is asking questions, then word might spread, and a revolution may take place."

"That's crazy," Mombassa said.

"Yeah, it is," Kingsmen replied. "Especially since everyone in the city knows that the Cigelians are there and that humans are prisoners out here with them."

"The Cigelians are NOT holding anyone prisoner," Mombassa said, this time her voice showing any politeness. They are the warmest, friendliest people I have ever met." She would have kept up the argument, but Chikelu started crying, so she had to leave for his two-hour feeding.

Kingsmen looked at the rest of the officers. "Look, my crew know I am here, and they know to be silent on the subject," he said. "If the president asks, and I know he will...I will tell him I found you checking out the plains north of here...out by the sulfur flows and that you cooperated with me and returned." They all thanked him, but then he had one more thing to add. "You must keep the captain and Chikelu out of sight for a while."

"I'll take care of that," Giovanni said. "I know just how to handle our captain."

Then, Ambassador Kingsmen saluted each person on the bridge and waited for Captain Mombassa to return before returning to his ship with one last order for Kiselow to follow his boat back to the Amelia Mary.

"Urulu, I have something to talk to you about," Giovanni started. "Ambassador Kingsmen suggested that you and Chikelu remain on the yacht when we return to the city." Mombassa started to say no but couldn't get a word out before Giovanni continued. "He said that they would most likely kill you and your son if you are discovered in the city."

"I will stay here with you, Urulu," Louis-Hart said. Kiselow and Asianne echoed that sentiment. I swear no one will harm you or your baby." Once again, the others confirmed what he said.

"I want to thank you all," Mombassa said. "It will be hard to explain why all our officers are missing." Then she looked at Louis-Hart. "Henry, I want you to stay with me. I know that you, no offense, will be the one who would best be able to stay and not be missed by the Terrans."

Louis-Hart laughed a little before he said..."Well, just a minor offense, but I know what you mean. I will stay, but I want them to check in every fifteen minutes." Mombassa agreed, and the order was given.

The Terran ship led the yacht back to the Amelia Mary and hovered above it until it was safely docked back in its berth, and the crew had exited the ship. As soon as their feet hit the ground, the crew was surrounded by armed troops. "Where were you?" the commander demanded to know.

"We were up north," Asianne answered. "Our science officer heard of volcanic sulfur flowing up there, and he wanted to do some research since we don't have anything like that back home."

"And just where is the doctor," the commander asked.

"He stayed behind for a couple of days to study the flows more," Asianne said. "As I said, he has never seen anything like that before, and he said that it would be important to learn all he could in case we ever find a planet like that when we travel outside the solar system."

"You had no dealings with the Cigelians," a second officer asked.

"Who," Giovanni asked. That got the officers upset…so upset that they ordered the officers escorted back to their rooms, and the Amelia Mary searched to see what they had with them. But before any of that could happen, Ambassador Kingsmen walked up and saw the guns.

"What's going on," he shouted at the Terran officers.

"I think they had dealings with the Cigelians," the first officer said.

"You know you are ignorant, don't you," Kingsmen asked. The officer shook his head as if he were afraid to answer. "These people are guests on Terra and are protected by the council and the president. So, I would suggest that you lower our guns and leave these people alone."

"Sir, the Cigelians," the officer said.

"Stupid, I found them up north at the sulphur flows," the Kingsmen said. They followed me back peacefully, so LEAVE THEM ALONE!!" The soldiers lowered their guns and backed away from the officers. "Come with me," the ambassador said as he took Asianne's arm and escorted them back to their hotel.

"I need to speak to the president and the council as soon as possible," Giovanni told the desk clerk as he walked past the desk. The clerk agreed to deliver the message, but the ambassador was confused and waited until they got up to the rooms to listen to an explanation. "I have a plan," the doctor said. "Whatever I do, I want you to play along and act like you don't know anything.

That night, Asianne was taken from her room and taken to a private meeting room in the basement. She sat down in a rather uncomfortable chair in a white room with dim lighting. "Please come in a sit-down," a voice said from a darkened corner of the room. I just have one question…where did you go earlier today?"

"We went to see some kind of geological feature Henry wanted to see," she replied. The voice asked if it was the geysers up on the eastern island. "No," Asianne answered. "It as some flow up north of here. We let him out to study them, and the air smelled sulfur. "Honestly, it makes me sick just thinking about how bad it was." The man left…he never got a straight answer but couldn't stay any longer without getting someone suspicious.

About an hour later, Doctor Giovanni was summoned to meet with the council. As she walked into the chamber, she didn't wait to be greeted before she asked her question. "I want to know right now…," she started. "…where is Captain Mombassa?" Then she walked up to the president and stood nose to nose with him. "I want her here right now, or I want to know what happened to her." Her voice became threatening, and even the president knew she meant business. "Well," Giovanni asked.

The president didn't take even a second to answer. "I have some bad news for you, Doctor," he said as the rest of the council sat quietly. "She went to check out a city in a distant land from here. The people there are not humans, and they despise humans, so they took her prisoner and executed her and her baby." Then, his chest swelled as he announced that they would seek revenge for the captain's needless death. "One thing I promise you is that we will get her body back for burial."

"Mr. President, I would like to thank you for that," Giovanni said. In the name of the Amelia Mary officers and crew as well as the people of Earth…again, I thank you." Then she got up and went back to the others at the hotel.

When Giovanni entered the door, Ambassador Kingsmen was in the room with Kiselow and Asianne. "Well, what happened," the ambassador asked before the doctor could take a seat.

Giovanni started laughing and asked a question of her own. "Did Urulu look healthy to you all," she asked. Each said she looked good, considering what she had gone through. That made Giovanni laugh even harder. It took her a moment to compose herself, but he reached for a glass of water the second she did, raised it over her head, and called for a toast.

"What else did they say," Asianne asked after taking a big sip of her drink.

"I didn't want to say anything yet, but Mostyn said that he is going to retaliate for the Urulu's death," Giovanni said.

"What does that mean," Kiselow asked. Now, he knew damn well what that meant, but he wanted…needed to hear the actual words spoken.

"He is going to launch a full military assault on the Cigelians, and it will not stop until there is no one alive in that village," Giovanni answered. Then she turned to Asianne, who told her to deliver a message to the captain about everything happening in the city and the threat against her friends. "That is too dangerous to talk about over the radio, so be quick and careful. We cannot let the captain be caught."

"I understand," Asianne said as she ran through the door and down the hallway. She was stopped and questioned several times but had already thought of an excuse. Each member of the ship's complement had a communicator, allowing them to read, write, speak, and understand any language they encountered. It was also necessary because the crew was multinational, so the translator was needed to get the ship working right. Her excuse was that every few days, the circuits in Amelia Mary's translator program had to be realigned to keep everything working just right. To emphasize the point, she threw in a couple of words from a movie she saw when she was a kid just to throw things off and verify the need for repairs.

The ambassador looked at the other officers with anger in his eyes. "He's going to do it," he said. "That megalomaniac is going to do it." He reiterated that the humans in that village were Terrans who either questioned or stood up to the president or the council. "I never thought he'd have the nerve, but now he has a reason to wipe them out."

"Get the rest of the crew and get them back on the Amilia Mary," Giovanni ordered. "Take some weapons and bring the babies back with you...all of the babies."

"What if the Terrans try and stop us," Asianne asked.

Giovanni didn't hesitate to answer; when she did, there was nothing...no feeling in her voice. "Shoot them," she said. "If they try and stop you and the crew or if they will not give you every baby born to our crew...shoot them and do not miss." It took about ten minutes before Giovanni heard the first of many shots fired. There was no way to tell if it was the Terrans or her people. "Get ready," she ordered as they started through the door. Ambassador Kingsmen led them down the hallway, into the lobby, and out to the street, where a bus was waiting.

"Get us to the aero port as quickly as you can," Kingsmen told the driver. It was about a thirty-minute drive, and when the bus pulled up, most of the crew and babies were standing outside the main door. The frightening thing was they were surrounded by soldiers with their weapons drawn and aimed at their heads. Kingsmen led them to the group and ordered the soldiers to stand down. "You know who I am," he told the soldier's commander. "I have the president's authority, and these people are protected."

"I do not know, sir," the officer responded. "I am supposed to hold them here if they tried to leave."

"Well, that order has been changed," Kingsmen said. His voice lost all sense of decency. "Lower your weapon and let them pass, or I promise you that you WILL regret your decision, and so will your family and their descendants for all time."

"I just got a message from the captain," Asianne said, interrupting the ambassador. "The Terran Command has just launched a dozen fighters, and they are headed toward the Cigelian settlement."

Giovanni looked at Kingsmen, and he looked back at her. Then he grabbed the soldier by the throat and placed him against the wall. "Soldier, I am not asking you…I am TELLING you lower your weapons and back off now." The look on his face was nothing short of the worst demon in Hell, but his voice and eyes were even scarier. "NOW!!!!" There was no question he was going to kill someone if his orders were not carried out at that second.

"Yes, sir," the officer replied. He was scared, and there was nothing but fear in his eyes and body. As the Kingsmen released him, he ordered his men to lower their weapons and back off five hundred meters. The men did as they were ordered, and while they did, the crew of the Amelia Mary boarded the ship with the babies in their arms. But not every crew member decided to leave. A few stayed behind to live on Terra.

Once the crew was on board, Kingsmen followed them, but a loud crack came from the field where the soldiers were standing, and the ambassador fell to the ground at the foot of the stairs.

"You bastards," Mombassa yelled as she saw her friend hit the ground. "Kiselow," she said with tears in her eyes. "Destroy that hill!"

The ship rumbled as a plasma missile lowered into firing position and fired. Just a second later, the bridge was filled with a bright white light. It was so bright that it gave everyone on the bridge a slight sunburn, but when it faded, the entire hill was gone.

"LAUNCH," the captain yelled.

"Vertical thrusters at seventy-five percent," Kiselow said. The ship rose smoothly into the air, and when it attained an altitude of five hundred feet, the captain ordered the course set for the Cigelian village to get there as fast as possible. Kiselow hit a button on his console, and the main engine came to life with a thunderous roar. The engines were at fifty percent a moment later, but they were still traveling more than thirty thousand kilometers an hour. "Captain," Kiselow said. "We will be at the Cigelian village long before the Terran ships."

"How long," Mombassa asked. He informed her they would be on-site at least three hours before the Terran ships. She must have been satisfied with that answer because she excused herself from the bridge and checked on Chikelu and the other babies.

Almost an hour later, the Amelia Mary reached the Cigelian village. By that time, all the babies were fed and sleeping, so Mombassa went back to the bridge and ordered Kiselow to place the ship no more than fifteen hundred meters above the treetops.

"Captain, Terran ships five thousand three hundred kilometers out," one of the bridge crew said. "Approaching at two thousand kilometers an hour." When the captain heard that, she asked how many ships were coming. "Sir, twelve fighters and three cruisers," he replied.

"Prepare the ship for battle," the captain told the bridge crew, who immediately relayed the order to the rest. The shields were raised within seconds, and the ship's weapons were primed and ready for battle.

"Captain," one of the crew said as she gazed at her computer screen. "The Terran ships will be here in less than ten minutes."

"Hail them on all frequencies," the captain ordered. Then she looked around the bridge. Janet, when they answer, I want you to talk to them and see what they say." Giovanni took the captain's chair as Mombassa moved to the back of the bridge. It took a couple of minutes, but finally, the Terran commander answered the hail.

"This is Doctor Giovanni in command of the Amelia Mary. Stop where you are," Giovanni said in a commanding voice. "The Cigelians are under our protection, and we will not allow you or anyone else to harm them."

"This is Captain Jorrisey," a voice said over the radio. "The Cigelians have killed your captain, and we have been sent to retrieve the body and punish those responsible for her death. Our actions are within Terran law and have been ordered by President Mostyn."

"Captain Jorrisey, do not come any closer…either return to base, or I swear we will stop you," Giovanni said. "We will retrieve our captain and take her home."

"Scan for weapons," Captain Mombassa whispered to Louis-Hart. He whispered back that although they may be able to put up a fight, the Terrans' weapons could not harm the Amelia Mary.

"We have our orders," Jorrisey said as one of the smaller ships started moving toward the village.

Giovanni didn't wait to see what it was doing. She ordered the Amelia Mary to position itself between the ship and the village. Once the boat took its position, they waited, but not for long. Within seconds, the bridge of the Amelia Mary was filled with the sounds of shots hitting the hull.

"That's it," Giovanni laughed as the fighters passed by the forward windows. She turned to Kiselow and ordered him to reduce weapon power to ten percent. When the fighter came in for its next pass, the doctor ordered Kiselow to fire.

A single missile flew from the launching bay directly under the bridge. A video display showed the warhead locked onto the fighter's exhaust. Despite maneuvers designed to avoid other Terran fighters, the missile, once it found its target, was not going to give it up. The entire flight only lasted seconds, and it ended with the sky filled with a blinding white light and the sight of the fighter falling to the ground.

"Captain Jorissey," a voice said through the Terran ship's comm system. "If you do not want to lose any more of your people, I recommend that you either stand down or return to base." The voice was not Doctor Giovanni's, so Captain Jorissey asked who he was speaking to. "This is Captain Urula Mombassa, commanding officer of the Amelia Mary, and I am telling you to back off right now, or you will be destroyed." To emphasize her statement, she ordered Kiselow to fire a shot into the hull of the closest cruiser. She saw the explosion and watched as the ship lurched to the right before recovering.

"Captain, hold your weapons," Jorissey radioed over. As he finished, the remainder of the fighters passed in front of the Amelia Mary's hull and then flew back toward the city, but the cruisers remained on station.

"Captain Jorissey," Mombassa began. "These people are protected, and I will not allow them to be harmed." Then she turned back to Kiselow and Louis-Hart and ordered them to set up a probe with a real-time feed to the ship's computer. That didn't take long, and it was placed in the village as soon as it was done. "CAPTAIN. DO NOT ATTACK THIS VILLAGE," she commanded. She never gave him a chance to answer. The Amelia Mary turned, fired her engines, and began the trip back to the city.

"Captain, the cruisers' position has not changed, and they have not fired on the village," Louis-Hart said.

"Urula," Giovanni said. "I don't think they know what to do, and I doubt their officers know how to handle anyone saying no to them."

"Well," Mombassa said. "Let's see what happens when we say no to Mostyn personally." She didn't tell anyone what that meant, and not one person on the bridge thought that she was going to, but she was angry, and that was not any way for a ship commander to be.

The cruisers didn't move as the Amelia Mary flew over the horizon. "Captain, you said that there were humans in that settlement," Giovanni said. The captain agreed, and then the doctor asked what she was going to do about them. "We can't just leave them there," she said.

"We aren't going to," Mombassa replied. Once we take care of business, we will go back and take care of them." Then she asked about the babies, especially Chikelu.

"They are all sound asleep and happy," Giovanni said. "Except for one, that is." There was a pause, and the doctor started giggling, which got the captain wondering. "Urula, we can't get Chikelu to shut up," she said between giggles. "He isn't crying or anything like that, but he IS laughing and cooing like crazy. He takes after you, Urula…you never manage to keep quiet either." That gave the bridge crew a good laugh, which they needed.

However, back in the Cigelian village, there was not much laughter. After all the years of peace and tranquility, having three Terran battle cruisers hovering above their heads was stressful.

"Urula said that we would be safe," Kathalonda reminded the council members beside her. "She would never leave us to face those ships alone." There was doubt among the people, but she kept reminding them that Captain Mombassa gave her word.

"I am not staying," a voice said from that back. Soon, the same sentiment spread from person to person. By the time it reached the entire community, more than five hundred humans and Cigelians had decided to leave the village and move out into the surrounding forests.

"Please stay," Kathalonda begged, but no one was listening to her...not any longer. It was so bad that even some Cigelian elders joined the group when they started to leave. However, as they moved off, one of the cruisers broke formations and followed them closely. Kathalonda didn't just stand and watch, though. She walked near the probe that Amelia Mary had left behind. "Urula," she said, hoping to get a response. "We have not been attacked, but our people are fleeing into the trees. I cannot do anything to stop them. What should I do?"

"Kathalonda," a voice returned from the probe. Tell your people I know what is happening, and I will be returning soon. I promise you will be safe."

Kathalonda returned and relayed the message to the remainder of her people, who, despite their misgivings, returned to as normal a life as they could.

"We have got to settle this," the captain told the bridge crew. "I am not going to let those people down." She scanned her monitors and ordered Kiselow to increase the ship's speed to nearly ten thousand miles an hour.

During the trip, the crew rushed to prepare the ship for a potential battle once they reached the city. Mombassa was not expecting or ordered to go into battle, but the situation had turned to the point where the choice may have been out of her control.

By the time the city was in view, the skies around the city and the Amelia Mary were filled with Terran fighters. Some of the fighters came within a couple of hundred feet of the ship's hull but did not show any aggression. Their mission was harassment to try and make the Amelia Mary fire first, and that was something Captain Mombassa was not going to do. She kept the ship at speed and on course toward the city's center. "Under no circumstances fire on those ships unless they make the first move," the captain ordered. The bridge crew acknowledged the order and went on with their business.

"Captain, Terran government offices twenty miles from our president's location," Kiselow stated. Mombassa told him to move within five miles of the building and hold that position. "Yes, captain," he responded.

"Urula, what are you up to," Giovanni asked.

The captain didn't answer... instead, she told Asianne to hail the Terran president. It was just a couple of seconds before her communications screen flickered to life, and she was face to face with the image of President Mostyn looking back at her. "Mr. President," she started. "I just want to tell you that rumors of my demise are just that...rumors." She hit the button to mute her microphone. "Henry, scan the council chambers," she said. "I want to know if anyone is in the chamber or the immediate area." The answer came back that the council chamber was empty, and there were no people anywhere in the area. She smiled at Louis-Hart and ordered him to lock several missiles in the council chamber and arm them fully.

"Captain Mombassa," Mostyn said with a mock surprise.

"Mr. President, we just came from the Cigelian village," Mombassa said. "You have ships waiting to launch an attack on the village, and I will not permit that."

"Captain, the Cigelian problem is OUR problem and has nothing to do with you or your ship," Mostyn said. "Now, you stand down and stay out of OUR business." He turned away for a second to talk to someone else in the room with him, and then the president turned his attention back to Captain Mombassa. "I just heard that you have kidnapped several Terran citizens."

"I have the babies of my crew if that is what you mean," Mombassa replied. They are citizens of Earth, and they belong to the women on this ship and no one else." President Mostyn began talking about Terran law, which concerned the babies, but the captain wasn't hearing any of it. She ordered the computer to break off communications with the Terran leader.

"Captain, the fighters are arming their weapons," Kiselow reported.

Captain Mombassa glanced over at Dr. Giovanni and then at the rest of the bridge crew. It was her moment, and she was ready for it. "Take them out," she ordered. "Destroy all of them!" *He wouldn't attack knowing the babies were on board...would he,* she thought to herself. Her question didn't take long to be answered as the closest of the fighters fired, just barely striking the plating on the hull. There was hardly any damage but a slight vibration across the ship as the shot hit. "Fire at will," Mombassa ordered, and before her sentence was finished, every gun the Amelia Mary had was aimed and fired. As the shots flew from the ship, the fighters exploded into balls of flame and fell to the surface.

"Twenty-seven down so far, captain," Kiselow said as more and more fighters were destroyed as they passed by the Amelia Mary.

"Lieutenant Kiselow, fire one shot into the council chamber," Mombassa ordered. "Set the charge at maximum. I don't want anything left of that room, but a voice came over the radio before Kiselow had the chance to follow the order.

"Urula, Terran forces have entered the village," the voice said. Mombassa recognized the voice immediately. It was Kathalonda, and she sounded scared.

"Captain, weapons at full," Kiselow said.

"President Mostyn, you just made the biggest mistake of your life," Mombassa said. Then he turned to Kiselow and ordered him to fire. A white-hot light left the bow of the

Amelia Mary, and a second later, an explosion rocked the capital city.

Black smoke filled the air, and windows shattered across the city. Thousands of people fell to the ground. The initial blast killed some, while others were shredded by shrapnel from broken glass and falling buildings.

"Reset," Mombassa ordered.

"Urula," Giovanni said as she gripped the captain by the shoulder. "That's enough. Those were innocent people."

Ignoring her, Captain Kiselow locked weapons on President Mostyn. "Mr. President, will you call off your forces and leave the Cigelians alone?"

"Captain Mombassa," a voice said on the radio. "President Mostyn is no longer in power; He has been arrested for endangering the Terran population." Mombassa was skeptical, but she listened anyway. "The forces have been withdrawn, and the Cigelians are safe." She waited a moment to hear anything else; whoever had to say

"Urula," Kathalonda's voice came across. "The soldiers have withdrawn, and the cruisers have pulled back out of the area."

"Are you sure," the captain asked. Kathalonda verified her statement and said the ships were well out of sight. "Lieutenant, keep those weapons armed and aimed." Then she asked the other voice who she was speaking to.

"I am Vice President Luthur Kingsmen," the voice. "I have taken control of the Terran government, and I promise you that the Cigelians are safe and will be under the protection of the Terran government."

"Captain," Kiselow said. "Those three cruisers are approaching from the north."

"Raise the shields and lock weapons on those ships." the captain said. Kiselow obeyed, but the ships, although they moved a half mile from the Amelia Mary, passed by without any signs of aggression.

"Captain Mombassa, can we meet," Vice President Kingsmen asked. Mombassa agreed even though she was still unsure of the Terran's motives.

The Amelia Mary landed back at the aero port, and once Captain Mombassa disembarked, guards were posted, and the ship was placed on red alert. Steps were taken to make sure that the babies were hidden and placed under heavy guard just in case the Terrans had any ideas of kidnapping any of the children.

Captain Mombassa was escorted to the president's office. She was driven past the former council chamber, where she saw rubble clogging and crews recovering bodies from the street. She kept her windows rolled because the stench of blood was so pungent that if she had even had one smell, she would have become unconscious within seconds. *It did not have to go this far*, she thought. *So much waste…so much waste.*

When her car reached the presidential office, President Kingsmen was waiting at the side of the street, awaiting her arrival. "Captain Mombassa," he said as she stepped off the ramp. Welcome back. I am looking forward to meeting with you and your officers."

"I hope this works out better than last," she replied.

"I promise you that it will," he said as he took her hand and walked her back into the terminal, followed by not only the officers of the Amelia Mary but also several armed guards. Together, they walked to the president's office, but as they walked, they passed the massive damage caused by Mombassa's attack. "I am sorry it had to come to this," the new president said. "We had no idea what Mostyn was doing. Maybe some of the government did know, but they didn't say anything. Mostyn's influence was that strong over the people here. I will change things so that something like this never happens again."

Mombassa had her doubts. In Earth's lifetime, so many spoke of peace while all the time planning for war. "What about the Cigelians and the exiled Terrans," she asked. "What about them?"

"They are citizens of this planet," Kingsmen replied. "I will bring them in, and they will be part of us. As a matter of fact...I want to meet with one of them while you are here...if you can arrange it?" The captain thought a minute, wondering if this was all for real. "Can you arrange it for me," he asked.

"Kiselow, take the yacht and bring Kathalonda back here and bring her to the president's office," the captain said. However, Lt. Kiselow had predicted her order and had already started back when she was done talking. It took a short time, but they watched the Captain's Yacht lift off and head toward the Cigelian community.

It was a four-hour trip to the Nigerian village. Kiselow explained what was happening, and not only Kathalonda but several elders decided to go back with her.

The sun started setting when the Captain's Yacht docked back with the Amelia

Mary. Kiselow unloaded the Cigelians and, as he was told, he escorted them to the president's office. Since Kathalonda and the others had never been to the city, they were nervous at everything they saw, but their nervousness was matched by the Terrans who lined the streets and had never seen a Cigelian. Very few of them even knew that another species was anywhere on the planet.

When they finally reached the office, Kiselow was the first to walk through the door. "Mr. President," he began. "Please allow me to introduce Kathalonda and the members of the Cigelian Council of Elders."

"I am honored to meet you," President Kingsmen said as he rose from his seat and greeted each guest. "Captain Mombassa has told me so much about you and your people."

"Captain Mombassa is respected among our people," Kathlonda said with a smile. "If she sent for us, she must believe that you are a good person, which is more than enough for us." President Kingsmen agreed that the captain was a unique woman and that he also trusted her when it came to the Cigelians. That was an excellent first step.

President Kingsmen invited Kathalonda and the others to take a seat. She took the seat closest to the president. "It is such an honor to meet you, Mister President," she said with a smile filled with friendliness and hope. She was quick to take her seat, and as she did, she took a bottle of clear liquid from her bag and some glasses from a nearby table and poured everyone a drink.

The drink was a form of wine made from a fruit on the Cigelian ship when it crashed. It was syrupy and sweet, but according to everyone in the room, it was delicious and gave each of them a feeling of euphoria. It was a little over an hour before their feelings returned to normal, and only then did the talks begin.

It only took a few moments for all involved to realize that the Terrans and the Cigelians wanted the same things…peace and the respect of the other species on the planet. However, by the time that first meeting finished, the Sun was coming up, so they broke off. The crew of the Amelia Mary was brought into the city, and they, as well as the Cigelians, were taken to a hotel to get some rest.

In the late afternoon, another meeting was planned, but this one would be different. The entire council would be there, and the meeting would be broadcast over every communication on the planet. President Kingsmen wanted to ensure that EVERYONE on Terra would learn of the Cigelians. It worked. People were talking and asking questions, and they wanted to know everything about their new neighbors. Captain Mombassa and her people observed, but they did nothing to interfere. Finally, Mombassa told her officers to pack up and return to the hotel.

In the morning, the captain and Kathalonda met at a restaurant next door to the hotel. "We are nearly done," Kathalonda said. "We have agreed on everything, and it will benefit both the Terrans and the Cigelians."

Captain Mombassa was happy about that, but after her coffee with Kathalonda, she walked to the president's office to congratulate him and ask him a question. "Mister

President," she said as he walked into his office. "I hear that thing went well." He acknowledged that the Terrans and the Cigelians had a good beginning, but it would take longer to complete everything. Then came the question. "Doctor Giovanni and Asianne would like to stay behind when we leave so they may study your people and the Cigelians. Do they have your permission to stay if they promise not to interfere in your world?"

President Kingsmen didn't have to think long before he gave his permission and actually praised the idea as a possible start to diplomatic relations between Earth and Terra.

"I believe that, too," Mombassa said, smiling because she hoped the three cultures would become friends and maybe more.

"Captain, while you have been here, we have placed something special aboard your ship," Kingsmen said. The captain didn't know what to say or what to ask, so she waited for him to continue. "We have built four probes…communication probes. Suppose you place them approximately seventy-two million kilometers apart on your journey. In that case, we will have full communication between your ship and us and be able to talk to and get to know the people of your world."

Although unsure if it would work, she agreed because Mombassa wanted this trip to benefit the people of Earth despite all the situations they had encountered.

After a private dinner with Kathalonda, the Kingsmen, and Captain Mombassa, she shook hands with the president, hugged Kathalonda, and started back to Amelia Mary. Along the way, she thought about the trip from Earth, the people she left behind, and the people she had met on Terra. For the most part, the thoughts were pleasant, especially when she thought of her time with the Cigelians. She had never felt like an actual human as when she was with people from another distant, alien world.

Giovanni and Arianne were waiting on the tarmac when Mombassa finally reached the ship. Neither of them said a word. It was as if they were showing her respect for royalty rather than being a spaceship captain.

"Janet, Asianne, are you having a good day," the captain asked.

Neither of them answered, but Giovanni said just one word…" Urula."

"Yes, Janet, Asianne…you will not be returning with us," Mombassa said. "As of now, your service aboard the Amelia Mary will no longer be required. I am ordering you to remain on this planet, research the peoples and cultures of Terra, and report back to the WSA regularly. Do you have any questions?" Both Asianne and Giovanni gripped the order. Both hugged the captain and backed away as she walked up the stairs to the hatch of her ship.

She cried as Captain Mombassa took her seat on the bridge and ordered the ship's engines to be ready for flight. "Lieutenant Kislow, let's get out of here and get back home," she said as she looked through the window and watched her two crewmates on the ground waving goodbye.

Slowly, Amelia Mary lifted into the sky. Once it reached an altitude of about a kilometer, the bow rose to an angle of seventy-five degrees, and the main engines fired. Within minutes, the ship was no longer in sight, and Amelia Mary was on her way to swing around Terra's moon.

"Urula, do you think we did all the right things," Louis-Hart asked.

The captain thought for quite a while before answering. "Kevin, I don't know if we did the right things," she said. "I do know one thing...," she said as she paused momentarily. "I know we gave the right thing a good start, but now it's on its own."

Everyone on the bridge agreed, but the conversation didn't last much longer...it was time for the babies to get some companionship. Chikelu was the first to be brought up. He was hungry but happy and smiled when the captain held him close to her. The rest of the babies were given to their mothers or, in the case of the babies who weren't wanted...either the male members of the crew took care of them, or one of the women would usually take care of more than one.

Throughout the trip, the officers and crew stayed active while the babies, except for when they were being played with or fed, were kept in stasis so their bodies would not be affected by space travel.

Finally, after months of travel, the Amelia Mary was hailed by a signal from its home planet. "Amelia Mary...Amelia Mary, this is W.S.A. Command. Can you hear us? " the voice asked.

"Command, this is Captain Mombassa of the W.S.S. Amelia Mary," Mombassa replied.

"Captain, where have you been?"

"We found it," she answered with pride in her tone. "We found the other Earth. It was right where we thought it was." Then she got some rather exciting news. W.S.A. Command had been getting some strange messages from a source they could not identify, even though whoever sent the messages knew about the W.S.A. and the Amelia Mary and even about the captain and crew of the ship. She explained about the Terrans and the Cigelians and how two of her crew members stayed behind to research their cultures.

"Captain," the voice said. There is a transmission coming in now." Mombassa told the voice to transfer the message to Amelia Mary.

Although the ship was still two days from Earth, the signal was strong. However, there was static, so Mombassa knew it would be hard to hear the message, but she ordered Kiselow to strengthen any signals beyond what he thought the receivers could handle.

A couple of minutes later, the first message came through the bridge. "Amelia Mary," a different voice said. "If you can hear this, I'm Doctor Giovanni from Terra. Amelia Mary, are you there?"

"Janet, this is the Amelia Mary…we can hear you," the captain replied. The one problem was that because of the distance between Earth and Terra, signals took several moments to make the round trip, so there was a delay in any answers. Mombassa paced back and forth around the bridge until an answer finally came in.

"Urula," Giovanni asked, but she didn't wait for an answer. "It is nice to hear your voice again." Then she just kept talking. "Everything is well here. The Terrans and Cigelians have a peace set up, and Cigelians have been welcomed into the city. Several of them have settled just outside the city limits."

"That is excellent," Mombassa said. "I am proud of your and Asianne's work." The signal died away as soon as she finished her statement, and Terra was lost.

Two days later, the babies were brought out of stasis for the final time. Their mothers and other crew members cuddled them while the ship entered the atmosphere. The reentry was smooth, and the landing took place without event. A couple of hours later, the hatches opened, and, for the first time in more than fifteen months, the members of the Amelia Mary tasted the air of their home world. One hugged and kissed while others dropped off their knees and kissed the tarmac, but the celebration didn't last long.

Within minutes, soldiers surrounded the crew. The babies were taken to a local medical center for examinations and observations. In contrast, the officers and crew were taken to a hangar, where they were briefed and debriefed. They were then briefed again before a medical checkup covering everything from hair follicles to toenail growth. Once the questions were answered and the crew was certified one hundred percent healthy, they were released and reunited with their families, including the new babies. Even the ones their mothers didn't want were adopted by other crew members and became members of their families.

Captain Mombassa was questioned more than other crew members. She was detained for more than six months, but not because of her last mission. She was being trained for a new mission.

The messages from Terra became increasingly positive, so the leaders of Earth decided to have another mission to Terra, but this time, it was not exploration. It was to set up diplomatic relations and trade, and it was to be a secret mission. So, she got her crew back, and on October 22nd, 2176, the Amelia Mary launched her second mission.

www.ingramcontent.com/pod-product-compliance
Ingram Content Group UK Ltd.
Pitfield, Milton Keynes, MK11 3LW, UK
UKHW031951131224
452403UK00010B/665